# THE HOT SPRINGS ON MOON MOUNTAIN

U0107912

FOREIGN LANGUAGES PRESS

First Edition 2023

ISBN 978-7-119-13189-4

© Foreign Languages Press Co. Ltd, Beijing, China, 2023

Published by Foreign Languages Press Co. Ltd.

24 Baiwanzhuang Road, Beijing 100037, China

http://www.flp.com.cn   E-mail: flp@cipg.org.cn

Distributed by China International Book Trading Corporation

35 Chegongzhuang Xilu, Beijing 100044, China

P.O. Box 399, Beijing, China

*Printed in the People's Republic of China*

# CONTENTS

东西

# Dong Xi

Dong Xi is the pen name of Tian Dailin. His novel *Record of Regret* was translated into English by Dylan Levi King and published by University of Oklahoma Press in 2018. His other novels include *Distorted Fate*, *Echo of a Slap*, *Life Without Words*, *Our Father*, and *Private Settlement*. He has received the Lu Xun Literature Prize, and is the chair of the Guangxi Writers' Association. Many of Dong Xi's works have been adapted for film and television, and he has been translated into numerous languages.

# 双份老赵

# Old Zhao Two-Times

## By Dong Xi

Now, don't get the wrong idea: Old Zhao wasn't that old. It was more like an affectionate title. He had the hair of a twentysomething and the complexion of a thirtysomething, and the wisdom of someone who had lived two lifetimes. He wasn't exactly carefree, though: since around the time he'd learned to read, he'd developed a sort of frown. He always looked like he was deep in thought. If you didn't know any better, you'd think he'd inherited it from his parents, but the permanent frown wasn't genetic, it was earned.

All of this takes place seven years back. There was a girl named Xiao Xia. She worked as bank teller. Xiao Xia was an elegant young woman, beautiful, and classy, too. There was no shortage of guys wanting to take her out. But Xiao Xia was looking for something in particular and, so far, none of these guys had that certain something. What she was looking for was: stability. The men that lined up for their chance with Xiao Xia all lacked a certain maturity. But, that day at the bank, when Old Zhao and his permanent scowl turned up on the other side of the glass, she knew that he was different. Her heart started thudding against her ribcage, right away. Her heart could thud all it wanted, but Old Zhao was only there to take care of his banking. After a while, though, Old Zhao and Xiao Xia got to know each other and got to talking. One day, Xiao Xia asked Old Zhao why he didn't put all his money in the account at her bank. He said, somberly: "It's not a good idea to put all your eggs in one basket, especially for a guy like me – the eggs are barely worth the baskets I've got them in."

The bank wasn't some fly-by-night operation, it was one of the most prestigious and reliable in the country. Even in a financial crisis, this wasn't the type of bank to go bankrupt. And Old Zhao's money was a drop in the ocean, for a bank like this. Xiao Xia thought he was being a tad overcautious. She wondered if he didn't trust her, but he reassured her: "I don't have a problem trusting one person, but an organisation, that's a whole different story." Xiao Xia's trust in the bank was complete and unshakeable. She trusted it as she'd trust her own father. Old Zhao said: "Just because you take a sip, it doesn't mean you have to suck down the whole cup, right?" Xiao Xia said: "Nothing comes between me and my company".

Old Zhao eventually relented and opened a savings account. Xiao Xia asked if he would be depositing all of his money into the single account. Old Zhao snorted in amazement and stifled a sneeze. He couldn't help himself. He started his lecture: "If you put your faith in one thing, and meet with disaster, you're ruined. An entire family should never get on one boat together. Or a plane, for that matter." At this Xiao Xia sneezed, too. She had finally found stability. This was a man as solid as concrete. But before she married him, a test was in order.

Xiao Xia spread out a map and pointed at a point on its margins: the Strait of Magellan. She said: "What do you think?" He said: "It doesn't matter, as long as you're happy. We can go next month." Her fingers danced over the map and landed on the Hawaiian Islands. She said: "Maybe somewhere a bit closer, if you're worried about money." Old Zhao slammed his fist against the table, causing the entire Pacific Ocean to wobble: "Are you making fun of me? You know what they say, you're bound to fall in love with whoever pays your way." Xiao Xia's fingers pliéd and then leaped up and across the ocean, landing like two white swans on a mountain peak in Guilin. "Then, let's go here," she said. Old Zhao's head was spinning. She changed her mind faster than he could keep track. Once he'd adjusted to the jet lag, he said: "When it comes to my money, spend to your heart's desire." Xiao Xia giggled: "I'll try to keep the budget under control. That's going to be my money someday."

They finally chose as their destination a mountain in the western part of the country. The peak was a famous sightseeing spot, called on by famous and respected visitors. A bigtime CEO was known for going there every quarter, trailing a group of journalists, and every time he went, the stock price of his company went up. Old Zhao thought it was a good choice. He wondered if going to the peak wouldn't do for his love life what it did for the CEO's stocks. Old Zhao and Xiao Xia both booked some time off work.

When Xiao Xia saw that Old Zhao had bought them both travel insurance, she felt a pang of happiness. As they waited for the flight to take off, Xiao Xia rested her cheek on Old Zhao's shoulder. She was sure she had made the right choice. Even when his shoulder and her cheek were both numb, neither moved; they stayed like that as the plane took off and were still in the same position when the plane landed.

As they were checking into their hotel, Xiao Xia realized that she had only booked one room. Old Zhao said: "Do you really think we need two rooms?" Xiao Xia pouted: "Of course! I have my principles." She didn't seem to be joking. Old Zhao went to the front desk to ask for a second room. The clerk told him: "These rooms all get booked up at least a week in advance." Old Zhao pleaded: "Could you put a cot in the hallway for me?" The clerk said: "We can't do that, but we could put a cot in the room." Old Zhao smiled broadly and turned and headed back to the room to tell Xiao Xia. She said: "I don't think I'll be able to sleep if you're here in the room, and if I can't sleep, I won't be able to hike up the mountain tomorrow." Old Zhao said: "We can't have that. You came here to relax."

Old Zhao and Xiao Xia went out for dinner and Old Zhao escorted her back to her room. She sat on the bed and he pulled up a chair. They started talking. Old Zhao was enjoying himself. He was babbling, even going red in the face. He looked like he could keep going until dawn. But Xiao Xia couldn't stop thinking about where Old Zhao was going to stay. Old Zhao suddenly said: "You know, maybe you didn't just accidentally forget to book an extra room. This was your plan all along, wasn't it?" Xiao Xia shook her head. She curled up on the bed, as if trying to get as far away from him as she could without rising from her place on the bed. Old Zhao said: "You really weren't hoping that we would stay together?" She lifted her head and nodded. Old Zhao asked

Illustration by Yuan Cong

again: "You're sure?" She nodded again. Old Zhao knew to ask twice but he also knew to take no for an answer. He picked up his suitcase and turned to go. As he opened the door, he called back: "Goodnight." Xiao Xia said: "Where are you going?" He said: "I'm going to sleep." She said: "You don't have a place to stay." Old Zhao said: "I was worried this might happen. Before we left, I called ahead to make sure I had my own room booked." Xiao Xia stared back at him, speechless. At that moment, she admired him… No, that word didn't go far enough: she worshipped him.

The next morning, they began their hike up the mountain. Old Zhao carried a rucksack and the pair both clutched bottles of water. Xiao Xia didn't have much experience as a hiker and quickly drained her bottle before they had reached the halfway point of the trek. Old Zhao told her that the correct way was to just wet your throat every now and then, rather than taking long pulls off the bottle. Xiao Xia said: "Why didn't you tell me earlier?" Old Zhao reached into his bag, pulled out another bottle of water and said: "Because I made sure to bring an extra bottle for you." As the path got steeper and rougher, Xiao Xia scratched her hand on a prickly shrub. Old Zhao inspected the wound and then reached into his bag for a Band-Aid. Xiao Xia said: "You thought of everything." Old Zhao said: "Of course."

Halfway up the path, they stopped and looked out from a crag on the countryside around them, and down at the distance they had already climbed. Their excitement rose and Xiao Xia insisted that she could make it all the way to the top. Old Zhao had helped her up this far but the path to the peak was treacherous and full of loose stones. Xiao Xia's feet slid out from under her a few times and, finally, she heard fabric tearing and realized she had split her pants. She said: "These were expensive." She squatted down and refused to take another step. She thought to herself: Old Zhao thought of everything but what about this? As she squatted on the trail, Old Zhao rummaged in his rucksack and pulled out a sewing kit. He passed it to her and she went to work stitching up the ripped seam. She asked herself: Is there any man in the world more reliable than Old Zhao? No, she answered, not a chance.

When they got back to the hotel that night, Xiao Xia told Old Zhao to cancel his reservation and spend the night with her. Now, everything seemed perfect but the trip ended on a sour note. The next morning, before they left, Old Zhao took Xiao Xia out shopping. She picked out a jade bracelet. The bracelet wasn't cheap but it was beautiful and it fit perfectly on her slender wrist. Before they left to get their flight back, Old Zhao excused himself and headed back to the shop where they had bought the bracelet. Xiao Xia caught him, when he got back, hiding in his luggage a bracelet identical to the one on her wrist. She knew that wasn't a good sign. He must be planning to give it to some other lover. Why else would he have gone behind her back and snuck back to the shop? She decided not to say anything. She had a plan: in a few weeks, she'd ask to see the bracelet, and if it was gone then that would prove there was another girl. No matter how clever he thought he was, she wouldn't listen to any of his excuses.

After they got back from the trip, Old Zhao mentioned marriage every three days, like clockwork. After the fifth time, she confronted him: "Tell me the truth and it'll go easier for you. Take that bracelet out, and maybe then we can talk about getting married." Old Zhao looked like he'd been caught stealing. Xiao Xia eyed him like a cat staring at a mouse: "Huh? You can't, huh? It's gone, isn't it? You gave it to your other girl, didn't you?" Old Zhao wiped the layer of sweat off his forehead and stammered: "Can't you let me keep this one little secret?" She said: "You want to keep secrets or you want to keep me? You gotta choose one."

Old Zhao turned and opened the cabinet above his desk. He took out the bracelet. Xiao Xia said: "Wow, you didn't send it to her yet? What are you waiting for?" Old Zhao said: "Who would I give it to?" Xiao Xia said: "Don't tell me you bought it just to keep it in this cabinet?" Old Zhao said: "I was worried that you would lose your bracelet or break it, so I bought an extra one." Xiao Xia felt a shiver run up her spine. She fought down the emotion and said: "Don't lie to me!" Old Zhao opened up the cabinet again and put the bracelet back inside. Xiao Xia caught a glimpse of what he kept in his cabinet: a cloth doll, high school and university diplomas, certificates, stamps, a photo album, a portable hard drive, keys, bankbook, insurance policy, bottle of heart pills, camera, watch. And there were two of each item… The only thing in the cabinet without an identical partner was the watch, and that was because Old Zhao already had one of them on his wrist. Xiao Xia stammered: "So-so-so you just like… You like collecting things?" Old Zhao shook his head: "I've had this secret for a long time. I held onto this secret as tight as a jockstrap. And I didn't expect that you would ever discover it. These are the things that I worry about losing. So, I made sure that I have two of everything. These things put my mind at ease."

At that moment, Xiao Xia felt twice as sure of herself as she had before. That winter, they got married. Old Zhao kept up his habit of buying two of everything. When he went out to get groceries, he brought back twice as much as they needed. After a while, Xiao Xia got tired of the wasteful habit. When she had to pour a jug of milk down the drain, she felt like a wicked capitalist. She couldn't help but picture the person that had milked the cow or the farmer that had stooped to pick the soybeans. She couldn't take it anymore. She forced herself to drink any milk that was going to be wasted. She ate and drank her fill and then kept going, hoping that nothing would go to waste. After a while, her stomach was swollen like a water balloon. She found it uncomfortable to sit and uncomfortable to stand. Her stomach began to hurt more and more. Old Zhao took her to the emergency room. She got some medicine and an injection and her stomach began to shrink back to its original size. When she was healthy again, she went to Old Zhao and said: "Aren't you worried about my health? We have to live together. You know what that means? It's not just about eating and drinking. It's about more than that. If you keep buying two of everything, you're going to be sleeping on the sofa."

Old Zhao promised that he would stop, but old habits die hard. Some nights, coming back home with the groceries, he would get to the front of their apartment block before realizing that he had once again bought two of everything. He ended up giving it away, pushing it on anybody that he could, whether he knew them or not, sometimes people just passing by. The compulsive gift-giving to strangers was just as odd as the habit of buying two of everything, and people in their neighborhood were becoming suspicious of Old Zhao. There were murmurs in the neighborhood that his gifts to local girls might come with strings attached. One night, coming home from the grocery store, Old Zhao found himself, once again, standing outside of the apartment block with twice as many groceries as he needed. A cold wind blew down the street. There was nobody around. He looked up to see a young woman coming out of the apartment building. He rushed over to her, trying to put the bags of groceries in her arms. The woman took a step back: "What? What is all this?" He said: "Help me. Please help me. I don't want my wife to know." The woman took a step forward: "You mean me?" The woman, Old Zhao realized, was Xiao Xia.

Xiao Xia was furious. She started confiscating Old Zhao's paycheck and she took away his shopping privileges. Old Zhao began moping around the house. He complained to her: "What should I do with my time?" Xiao Xia said: "Why don't you start jogging?" Old Zhao said: "I'll never run faster than Liu Xiang, so why bother?" After dinner, he spent the evening on the sofa, watching TV. After ten nights, the sofa bore the grooves of his ass and elbows. Xiao Xia said: "Have you ever thought about being a father?" He said: "Of course! Every time I hear a kid calling for their dad, I whip my head around." Xiao Xia said: "You'd better start looking after your seed, then." He jumped up from the couch. Finally, he thought, something to do. He went out and ran two kilometers. After a few nights of running, he thought that the mother of his future child should be as healthy as the father: a good seed needs fertile soil. He brought her out running with him. In their free time, they played badminton, did calisthenics, and went swimming and biking. Anyone that witnessed their training program might have thought that they were training for a pentathlon rather than getting ready to have kids.

They consulted school enrollment dates and astrological signs to decide the best date to conceive, and then, with the concentration of technicians preparing for a rocket launch, they set about preparing for the moment. But at the last minute, Old Zhao had second thoughts. Xiao Xia asked: "What are you waiting for? You need an invitation?" Old Zhao said: "I want to have two. I need two kids." Xiao Xia said: "Rules are rules: we can only have one."

Old Zhao said: "No. We can't let that limit us. We can have twins." Xiao Xia asked: "Why does it have to be twins?" Old Zhao said: "If we only have one kid, just think... There are so many dangers: car accident, disease, natural disaster, the kid could be accused of a crime and thrown in jail... If we have twins, it's less to worry about." Xiao Xia felt a shiver run up her spine. She took her husband in her arms: "I want to have twins, I really do. But for now, let's finish this." Old Zhao rolled on a condom, thought for a moment and rolled on another. Xiao Xia said: "Is that really necessary? When you go out do you put two socks on each foot?" He said: "No, but if I get a hole in my sock, it's no big deal. If one of these condoms is defective, we'll lose our chance to have twins."

They continued their program of physical fitness and Xiao Xia started taking fertility medication. The medication would help increase their chances of having twins. With all those hormones in her bloodstream, there was a better chance that, when Old Zhao sent his shots downrange, he would be firing at two targets. But things did not turn out as Old Zhao and Xiao Xia hoped: a year later, when Xiao Xia gave birth, it was to just the one daughter. Old Zhao and Xiao Xia loved their daughter. In the first weeks, the only place she slept was in their arms, passed back and forth between them. Old Zhao's old habit of buying two of everything seemed to have been broken. Instead, he did his best to save money. It seemed that their daughter had cured him of his illness.

Their daughter grew up fast. The only other thing shooting up as fast as her was the price of houses in the city. The money that could have paid for an apartment on the day she was born wouldn't cover a single room by her third birthday. Xiao Xia came to Old Zhao one day and asked: "What do you plan to leave behind for your little girl?" Old Zhao was at a loss: "It's not time to talk about that yet, is it? I'm going to be around for a while." Xiao Xia said: "She'll need a place to live, at least. Have you thought about that? We should think about buying an apartment." Old Zhao said: "Hey, I'd love to buy an apartment, but we just don't have the money." Xiao Xia held her hands out in front of her, her palms cupped like a beggar. Old Zhao recoiled from her. He said: "We don't have the money! I'm telling the truth." Xiao Xia said: "What about your other bank account? I saw the bank book in your cabinet." Old Zhao said: "You're not playing fair. Look at how much I've improved, you saw what I bring home from the store now. You should be giving me back my paycheck to reward me, not making more demands of me!" Xiao Xia said: "The price of apartments is only going up. If we don't jump into the market now, we won't be able to scrape up enough to make an offer on a washroom." Like some eager, sex-starved lover, Old Zhao crumbled under the pressure after putting up a token resistance. He handed over his bank book. Xiao Xia added up the totals in all of their accounts and handed the bank books back to him. She said: "Find an apartment. Make the down payment with this and get a mortgage for whatever's left." In a matter of days, Old Zhao had picked out an apartment and had it renovated. With an apartment and a mortgage, they could rent the place out and bring in an income, and, in the future, they would have an asset that they could pass on to their daughter. No longer would they be the kind of people that bitch and moan about the price of houses going up – they would probably never use a word like "bitch" in polite society again, now that they had joined the ranks of the property owners.

One day, while tidying up the house, Xiao Xia peeked into Old Zhao's cabinet and discovered that all of the things he kept there had been stripped of their partners: there was one camera, one copy of each of his diplomas, and so on. She asked him where the things went. Old Zhao said: "I had to sell some things to make up what I was missing from the down payment, and the rest of the things, I just tossed." Xiao Xia was skeptical. Once Old Zhao was out of the house, she searched high and low for the missing items. When she couldn't find them, she became even more curious. Finally, after ripping open every drawer, cupboard and hidey-hole in the house, she found something: freshly cut keys, stuck to the back of a cupboard with glue. She ripped them free and rushed out the door.

Xiao Xia had not been to the new apartment since the refurbishment. She hated the smell of the glues and varnish that the decorators used, and she was too busy looking after their daughter, anyways. She slammed the key into the lock and battled to twist it open. Maybe the lock was stiff or maybe she was shaking too much but it took three tries to unlock the door. When the door swung open, she found herself looking into a room identical to the living room in their own apartment. Everything in the living room, down to the color of the drapes, was identical.

If she hadn't known better, she might have thought she had somehow stumbled back into her own place. She took a few steps into the apartment and saw that the rest of the apartment was a mirror image of her own home, as well. The refrigerator was the same model, the cabinets in the kitchen were the same, too, and even the things in the drawers were about the same as the things in her own drawers. The guest bedroom was the same, too, and so was the office. She opened up the cabinet above the desk and saw the things that had disappeared from

Old Zhao's cabinet: the doll, the diplomas, the photo albums, the camera... Old Zhao had brought all of those things, here.

The door to the master bedroom was shut. She tried the handle but it was locked. She stood in front of it, looking for the key that would open it. The door swung open, and Xiao Xia took a step back. The door had been opened by her twin, or at least a woman that could have been her own sister. Both women had the feeling that they were looking into a mirror. There was a pause. The gaze of each woman fell to the left wrist of the woman standing across from her.

*Translated by Dylan Levi King*

毕飞宇

# Bi Feiyu

Bi Feiyu was born in Xinghua, Jiangsu province in 1964, and graduated from Yangzhou Teachers' College in 1987, where he studied Chinese Literature. He has worked as a teacher, a news reporter, and a literary editor. He is now professor at the Bi Feiyu Creative Writing Workshop at Nanjing University. He started writing in the 1980s, and is the author of eleven volumes, including the novels *Moon Opera*, *Three Sisters*, and *Massage*. He is the recipient of the first and third Lu Xun Literature Awards, the fourth Man Asian Literary Prize, and the eighth Mao Dun Literature Prize. His works have been translated into over twenty languages.

# 大雨如注

# The Deluge

## By Bi Feiyu

## 1

The lass took after neither the mother nor the father – how *did* she come out so good looking? A crude joke went around the compound: "Dayao, she's no seed of yours." Dayao could hear the approval behind the crudeness, of course, and never lost his temper. Unruffled, he'd respond: "Genetic transplant."

Dayao was a plumber, but he was a plumber at a teacher's university, so naturally his diction was elevated. He was careful in his speech – he'd known plenty of professors, and even more plumbers, and in this day and age what real difference is there between a plumber and a professor? None at all, you might think. But there is one crucial difference, and it is located in the mouth. Different speech issues from different mouths, and so different pockets are filled with different gold. The tongue is a soft thing, but it holds a hard power.

Dayao, like his father, was no fool. Like any father he was happy to hear his daughter's beauty praised, but of course he hoped the praise wouldn't stop at her beauty. "She's passable," he'd say. "It's more a matter of her bearing." His nonchalance was disingenuous; he threw everything he had into elevating their compliments to a higher level. There's two kinds of talk, they say, that should always be taken with a grain of salt: a mother's praise for her son, and a father's for his daughter. They may appear calm, but inside they're burning up.

Of course Dayao wasn't wrong about his daughter's bearing. When Yao Zihan was only four her mother, Han Yuejiao, began her training. First was dance class – ethnic dance. Dance is a queer thing, it can take root in a child's bones, and raise them up. What does "raise them up" mean? It's hard to say, but you know it when you see it. A firm axis ran from Yao Zihan's waist up through her back, and into her neck, and it never for a moment left her.

She had many hidden talents, as well: She'd played *go* for four years, and was ranked. She had a lively Ou-style calligraphy. She could sketch accurately. She could do paper-cuts. She'd placed second in the municipal Math Olympics. She excelled at public speaking. She could program computers. She'd performed *guzheng* solos on the provincial Spring Gala program. Her English was particularly strong, and spoken with an American accent. When she said "water" it never came out as *wo-te*, but always the proper *wa-te-er*. Yao Zihan's full array of skills far outstripped the ancient cultured requisites of chess, zither, calligraphy, and painting. Yao Zihan's strengths were best displayed in mathematics: her scores had always remained comfortably within the top three of her class, and top ten of her year. It was uncanny. Her second year classmates at the elementary school had long since stopped seeing her as one of them. They weren't jealous, quite the opposite: they took pride in her, and called her "Painted Skin," after the beautiful monster of legend. But it went deeper than that. When she stood she rose with elegance; when she sat she was enthroned. She was the very figure of grace, the very image of an arty youth. The dean had seen every type of child under the sun. Never mind "Painted Skins," he'd known zombies and goblins, too. But to be honest, not one of those zombies or goblins had developed in as balanced or well-rounded a way as this Painted Skin. The dean once cornered her in the library, and asked in the reverent tones of a die-hard fan: "Where on earth do you find the time and energy?" "A girl's got to be hard on herself," she'd replied with the self-possession of a true teen idol.

And Yao Zihan was extremely hard on herself. From the moment she became a young woman, she hadn't wasted a single hour of daylight. As with most children, it began with her parents pushing her. But in truth, whose mother or father *isn't* hard on their children these days? Any parent picked at random would make a perfect prison warden. But in the end, of course, most kids can't handle it: push them too hard and they'll bite back sooner or later. Yao Zihan was different, though. Her ability to endure was akin to the sponge from Lu Xun's story, that was squeezed dry by an iron hand: squeeze a little harder, and there's yet another drop of water to be had. At a parent teacher meeting Dayao had once complained: "We keep reminding Yao Zihan that she should rest, but she won't listen!" What could you do?

## 2

Michelle was very punctual. At precisely ten-thirty in the morning she presented herself in the Yao family living room. Dayao and Michelle had met under interesting circumstances: in the women's restroom of the library. Dayao had been fixing a spigot in the sink when Michelle had come barging in, a cigarette clamped in her jaw. Before she could light her cigarette she noticed a tall man standing there. She jumped out of her skin, blurted a mangled "sorry" in Chinese, and ran out. A few seconds later, however, she came strolling back in. She leaned against the doorframe, the cigarette trailing from her right hand at shoulder-height, and said archly, "Hey huntsome, are you looking for a taste?" How did this foreign girl know a phrase like that! Dayao said, "I don't eat in the restroom, and I don't smoke in the restroom, either." As he spoke he pointed to his uniform, and knocked on a water pipe with the wrench in his hand – the misunderstanding was promptly cleared up. Michelle was a bit embarrassed. She crumpled the cigarette in her palm and said, "Yours truly made a mistake." Dayao laughed. She was an American girl, healthy and self-confident, probably in her early twenties. Still girlish, and a little vain. "A good comrade learns from her mistakes," Dayao said. Once two people have met, they're sure to meet again. After the restroom incident Dayao and Michelle ran into each other four or five times, and each time Michelle seemed thrilled to see him; she'd call out to him loudly: "huntsome!" Dayao, for his part, would give her a thumbs-up, and answer "good comrade." Just before the summer vacation began, Dayao saw Michelle walking past a crêpe stand. He squeezed his brakes, set one foot on the ground, blocked her way, and asked her outright if she had any particular plans for the vacation. Michelle told him she would stay in Nanjing, and volunteer at a Kunqu opera theater. Dayao had no interest in Kunqu, he said: "I want to discuss a bit of business with you." Michelle arched an eyebrow, and rubbed the tips of three fingers together: "You mean, *bazness* bazness?"

"That's right," Dayao said. "Business."

Michelle said, "I've never had done bazness before."

Dayao wanted to laugh. Foreigners all talked like that. They added "had" to everything. He didn't laugh, though. "It's a simple thing. I want you to have a conversation with someone I know."

It took a moment, but Michelle understood – someone must need to practice speaking English.

"With who?"

"With a princess."

These poor Americans, they can never keep a problem inside their heads: all their wondering and pondering is right there on their faces for anyone to see. One eyebrow and the corner of her mouth thought for a while, and then Michelle realized what "princess" meant. She spoke in intentionally exaggerated "foreign-devil" Chinese: "Your royal highness, I understand-a!"

But then she wrapped her arms around her waist and glared at Dayao, her chin and gaze slowly shifting in opposite directions. She put on a crafty look, and said, "I'm very expensive, you understand-a?"

Dayao knew the prices, of course. He low-balled: "Eighty an hour."

"One hundred and twenty," she said.

"One hundred." Dayao said. He added, meaningfully: "The yuan is very valuable these days. Deal?"

Of course Michelle knew the yuan was very valuable. One hundred just for an hour of talking was a good price. She flashed a toothy smile: "Why not!"

Standing in their living room, Michelle looked as cheerful as ever. She was excited and kept rubbing her hands; this made her appear to take up even more space, and the living room seemed smaller. Dayao formally introduced her to the princess. During the summer vacation following elementary school, the princess had been given excellent training in social niceties, and her comportment was excellent, proper and noble. She was somewhat expressionless, though, as if Michelle crowded her. Dayao had noticed that his daughter's face rarely betrayed any expression, as though it were disconnected from her thoughts and feelings. She bore a perpetual look of disinterested amiability. The princess, solemn and noble, ushered Michelle into her sanctuary, and Dayao closed the door behind them, leaving it a crack. He wanted to listen, all the more so because he could not understand. What greater sense of accomplishment could a father have than to hear his daughter speaking a language he does not understand? He relished it; the world was vast and full of marvels.

Dayao took a moment to signal to his wife with his chin. Han Yuejiao, a gardener at the teachers' university, took the hint immediately. She donned her sleeve guards and started making dumplings. The couple had planned things the night before: they would treat the American girl to a meal. Both Dayao and his wife were canny; they never made a

Illustration by Wang Yan

losing deal. They calculated thusly: they were paying Michelle for one hour of language instruction, but if they could get her to stay for dinner afterwards, their daughter would get two.

Dayao had been pondering the question of his daughter's spoken English for a long time. Her English was excellent, there was no question – her midterm and semester test results were proof of that. But one day last year, as he was eating lunch, Dayao happened to glance at the television, which was showing a middle school English competition. As he watched he suddenly realized – Yao Zihan's "excellent English" only went as far as the eye and hand, not the tongue. To put it another way, it wasn't "hard power." Dayao and Han Yuejiao watched the program together. As luck would have it, they got addicted. As highly-experienced consumers of television, Dayao and Han Yuejiao were like everyone else in the country: their favorite thing to watch was something called "PK." This is the age of the PK, the "player kill," the utter annihilation of one's opponent. Singers PK, dancers PK, pianists PK, public speakers PK, even blind daters PK, so of course English speakers PK, too. On the day of the children's English PK finals, Dayao came up with a new set of "good girl" standards and requirements for Yao Zihan. Simply put, they were these: One, to get on television. Two, to withstand being PK'ed. Stated a little more clearly: the child who went through the PK and was still standing at the end was the truly "good child." Those who fell would at best be considered "revolutionary martyrs." That night, Dayao and Han Yuejiao began drawing up their plans. Their thinking went as follows: Due to an oversight on their part, Yao Zihan had had no spoken English training during elementary school, and if she were to suddenly be thrown into a competition now, as a middle-schooler, she might not even make it through the elimination round. But that mattered little – so long as Yao Zihan began cramming in early middle school, by the time she was in high school three or four years later, she'd be able to tell her moving story on the television; she would do her parents proud. As she imagined this scene of her daughter "doing her parents proud," Han Yuejiao's heart swelled and broke, and her eyes swam with tears. She and her daughter had been through so much, so much . . . truly they had been through so much.

At about the same time Michelle emerged from Yao Zihan's bedroom, Han Yuejiao was setting the table for the dumpling dinner. Han Yuejiao had never before had direct contact with "foreign friends," and she was feeling embarrassed. Embarrassment can often come out as brusqueness, and she said to Michelle: "Eat! Dumplings!" Dayao noticed that Michelle seemed as nonplussed by the steaming plate of dumplings as she had been the day he surprised her in the restroom – her face had flushed red. Michelle spread her long arms wide and said, "How could I possibly?" Hearing that, Dayao immediately assumed the role of foreign diplomat; it was his responsibility to clarify the stance of the Chinese. He told Michelle, in tones of great gravity: "The Chinese people are very hospitable."

"Of curse . . . of curse." Michelle answered, equally grave. "Of curse."

Michelle was in a bind, however. She had dinner plans. She hesitated. In the end she was swayed by the rising steam – she pulled out her phone, and told her friend that she was going to have a small meeting with three Chinese people, and she would have to arrive a bit later. Ah, so this American girl could lie – and even her lies were delivered in authentic Chinese style.

The dumpling banquet, however, was not a joyous one, mainly because it did not develop according to Dayao's plans. Before the meal officially began, Michelle delivered a whole speech's worth of polite courtesies, all in Chinese. Dayao glanced at his daughter, trying to give her a hint. Yao Zihan, sharp as a needle, *of course* caught his meaning. She picked up the thread of Michelle's conversation immediately, in English. But Michelle gave Yao Zihan a brilliant smile and encouraged her to "use Chinese," pointing out that "in her own home" it was "impolite" to speak a foreign language in front of her parents. Michelle was careful to be modest, of course, saying: "I also want to learn Chinese from you."

Dayao hadn't seen this coming. He'd paid for Michelle to speak English with his daughter. Yet now his daughter was speaking Chinese with Michelle, and not only was it free, she was getting a dumpling dinner as part of the deal. How had this happened?

Han Yuejiao shot a look at her husband. Dayao caught it. Naturally it was a look filled with import. Not accusation, exactly, but certainly a degree of disappointment, and Dayao blamed himself.

The moment Michelle was gone Dayao went nuts. He wanted to curse, but couldn't bring himself to do it in front of Yao Zihan. His taciturn daughter had a constant deterrent effect on him, which he resented, and resentfulness magnified his suffering. After more than ten years of working in an academy of higher education he'd learned to frame his suffering within a larger context, and in tones of great pain he said to Yao Zihan, "The weak nation has no voice – why must it always be we who are cheated?"

Han Yuejiao only stared emptily at the few remaining dumplings. The roiling steam was gone and the dumplings lay like corpses, unappealing. But Yao Zihan turned away from them and began fiddling with her computer and television. Within moments, scenes of her conversation with Michelle suddenly appeared on the television, and she was able to fast-forward, reverse, and replay them. Yao Zihan, the tireless student, had recorded the whole thing so she could study it afterwards as often as she pleased.

Dayao stared at the screen, elated. It was the kind of joy particular to the downtrodden, when at last they're able to take some small advantage. His mood reversed so quickly and so thoroughly that his joy was also magnified, almost hysterical. Dayao clutched his daughter tightly, and said stiffly: "Our motherland thanks you!"

## 3

Dance class was at seven that evening. Yao Zihan wouldn't let her mother take her. She got on her bike and set out alone. Though Han Yuejiao was ostensibly employed as a gardener, she was essentially idle, and her only real duty and pleasure was to accompany her daughter to her classes. When she was younger Yao Zihan had little say in the matter, and by this point Yuejiao had become accustomed to the routine; it was she who needed it now. But at the start of that year's summer vacation, Yao Zihan's face had told them in no uncertain terms that they were no longer allowed to accompany her. Dayao and Han Yuejiao were like any parents: their daughter may be essentially expressionless, but they could still tell from her face what they were supposed to do.

A chill breeze was blowing. Yao Zihan rode her bicycle, her emotions torn. She'd forbidden her parents from accompanying her because she was resentful, and angry at them. Any type of dance would have done – why couldn't her mother have chosen International Standard Ballroom Dance? Yao Zihan had only recently fallen under the spell of

"ISBD." ISBD was cool; each movement quick and sharp, electrifying. Yao Zihan had fallen in love with it instantly. She'd asked her teacher if there was still time to switch to ISBD, but his answer was vague – it wasn't *impossible*. But that was the thing about movement: once you'd trained past a certain point it took root in you, and the harder you'd trained the more difficult it was to make the switch. Yao Zihan had tried a few of the ISBD movements in front of the big mirror, but couldn't get them right. They were too graceful, too gentle. What you'd expect from a "little woman."

Then there was the *guzheng*. Why on earth had they picked the *guzheng* for her? When had that started? Yao Zihan had recently become infatuated with being "cool," and developed a distaste for anything that was visually "uncool." Yao Zihan had once performed in a school concert, and afterwards took a look at the recording. She looked gormless compared to the others. A *guzheng* performance wasn't even as impressive as the *di* flute, not to mention the sax or piano. Embarrassingly earnest, and totally uncool. Yao Zihan cut too miserable a figure to appear onstage.

The evening wind lifted her short hair and made her squint. What Yao Zihan felt wasn't just resentment, wasn't just anger. She hated them. Was this what they called taste? Was this what they called vision? Meanwhile all the drudgery had been hers. Not that she minded drudgery, if it was worth it. What she found most depressing was that she'd progressed too far to give it all up now. But she felt cheated. Big time. If only she could just start her life over again, and be her own boss, make her own decisions. Just look at her: her life was obviously off-track but she couldn't hit the brakes. She couldn't even let up on the accelerator. It was nuts. What greater sorrow could life hold? Yao Zihan suddenly felt old; in her imagination the crow's feet were piling up at the corners of her eyes.

In the end it all came down to one thing: money. Her family was too poor. If they had money, her parents' decisions might have been different from the start. A piano, for instance: they couldn't afford one. Even if they could it wouldn't fit in the house, just finding a spot for it would be a problem.

If you got right down to it, though, the problem of money had always been secondary, the real issue was her parents' taste, and vision. Yao Zihan's sense of humiliation welled up again. Her classmates all knew Yao Zihan's home was in the "big yard" of the teachers' university. That sounded good, as far as it went, but Yao Zihan never went into any more detail. In fact, her parents were peasants from the distant edge of town. It had been the relocation and expansion of the teachers' university that had allowed Mr. and Mrs. Dayao to transform themselves overnight from a young peasant couple to university staff members. That transformation had cost Dayao's father no small amount of cash.

It is the nature of humiliation that it can lead to self-pity. Yao Zihan, that renowned Painted Skin, that encyclopaedic giant, pitied herself profoundly. It was all completely meaningless. Through all that suffering and hardship she'd accomplished nothing but to lay the wrong-headed foundations of a wrong-headed life. It was too late to go back.

Thank god for "Her Royal Highness." "Her Royal Highness" was in the same dance class as Yao Zihan, a goblin-grade boy from No. 21

Middle School. He was actually quite macho, but the girls in the dance class insisted on calling him by his nickname. HRH didn't mind, he just gave a red-lipped, white-toothed smile.

Yao Zihan and HRH weren't friends for any particular reason, besides the fact that they had similar problems. People with similar problems might not be able to comfort each other, but just being together can often be reassuring. HRH had told Yao Zihan that his greatest wish was to invent a time machine, in which all the children no longer belonged to their parents. Instead, they would be their own masters, and could choose their fathers and mothers as they pleased.

Yao Zihan and HRH walked their bikes back from class, chatting for a few minutes along the way. Just as they were reaching the intersection, as they were about to part, Dayao and Han Yuejiao appeared and blocked the way. The two of them were squeezed awkwardly onto one electric bicycle, and looked peculiar. The moment she saw them Yao Zihan was unhappy – hadn't she told them not to accompany her? Yet here they were.

At this particular moment, however, she wasn't the only unhappy one. She hadn't attended very carefully to her parents. If she had, she would have seen that Han Yuejiao's face was severe, and Dayao's expression could be described as distorted.

He squeezed the brakes of the bike, and said with no preamble: "What do you mean by this?"

"What do I mean by what?" said Yao Zihan.

"What do you mean by not letting us accompany you?" he said.

"What do you mean what do I mean by not letting us accompany you?" she said.

Dayao dropped this pointless back-and-forth and went to the heart of the matter: "Who gave you permission to talk to him?" Without giving Yao Zihan a chance to answer he repeated the question: "Who gave you permission to talk to him?"

Yao Zihan looked at her father – she still hadn't really understood what he meant. Dayao retained a grip on himself, but it wasn't a very firm grip, and he could lose it at any moment.

Just as in the classroom, where Yao Zihan didn't need the teachers to ask a question more than twice, she understood what her father meant. She pushed her bicycle forward, saying quietly: "Excuse me, please let me pass."

Compared to Dayao's thunderous power, Yao Zihan possessed at the very most four ounces of strength. But that was the miraculous thing: those mere four ounces were enough to let her simply walk through the thunder. She was as cool as pure bottled water; as noble and self-possessed as a princess, and just as condescending.

The daughter's arrogance and haughtiness was enough to kill the father. Dayao barked, "That's the end of your dance classes!" It was nonsense, of course; he'd simply lost control.

Yao Zihan had already quietly passed by the electric bike. She suddenly turned back, this time she looked nothing like a princess – on the contrary, she was a scolding shrew. "I'm tired of it anyway!" she said, her pretty face flushed red. "Send me to ISBD classes, if you can afford it!"

Yao Zihan disappeared beneath the streetlights, and Dayao did not pursue her. He propped his electric bike up by the side of the road. He was calming down. But calm sorrow is the most painful. Dayao gazed at his wife, like a fish newly out of water, his mouth opening and closing. His daughter had finally broached the subject of money – it had only been a matter of time before she said what was really on her mind. As the lass grew older she was increasinly humiliated by her family's poverty, increasingly contemptuous of them as parents, Dayao could see that plainly. He could feel it – in the first half of the year alone she'd concealed two parent-teacher conferences from him. He hadn't dared ask; it had made him angry, but even more it had made him ashamed. Shame is a very peculiar organ. It's full of veins and arteries, just below the surface, and turns into a bloody mess at the slightest touch.

Dayao felt sad, but more than that he was bitter. Bitter not only about what all those years had cost him, but because there was a secret behind that bitterness: Dayao wasn't rich, but his family was. That's an awkward statement – Dayao really didn't have much money, but his family did.

How did his family come to have money? That was a long tale to tell, one that started in the year of Yao Zihan's birth. It was at once strange and relatively common: the teachers' college needed land. And the moment the teachers' college needed land, Dayao was elevated to a Buddha before he could say *amitabha*. This was a strange age, Dayao felt, and an even stranger land.

Mostly it was thanks to Dayao's father, Laoyao. The clever old peasant had discovered, long before Dayao was even married, that the city was like a pizzle on its wedding night: it was big, and getting bigger, and would eventually knock up against their own front door. Their house

Illustration by Wang Yan

was built on foundations of gold: if the teachers' college didn't buy it, the University of Science and Technology would; if an institute of higher education didn't buy it, a property developer would. In a word: there would be a buyer. Of course, plenty of people besides Laoyao knew this secret. Everyone had figured it out. The problem is that as people survey their future prospects they tend to get greedy, to lose their patience, and to pounce on their perceived gains. But the moment they pounce, they lose their position. He told his son: don't go anywhere. Whatever you might be able to grasp is just petty cash, you're waiting for the big one. Earning money by the sweat of your brow is a mug's game – have you ever seen the wealthy sweat? You just sit tight. He put a firm stop to his son's imbecile plan to buy an apartment in the city, and refused to let him shift his housing registration, either. He instructed his son to stay put in Yao Village on the outskirts of town, and then to build, slowly and steadily. And finally to grit his teeth and wait. "Do you really think," the old peasant would say, "that rich people earned their own money?"

Dayao's father bet correctly, and his plots of land won him big money. It was no small winning, either – it was a proper, respectable chunk of cash. The old man didn't let it go to his head, though. He handed over everything he'd made to his son, then made three pronouncements to the couple. 1) Nothing we do in life means anything, except what's done for our children. As your father I've made you wealthy; I've done my part. 2) Don't show it off. You're not a businessman, so live as if you were still poor. 3) The two of you are parents, too, and you've got to provide for *your* children. But just sitting and waiting isn't going to work for their generation. You've got to find a way to send that child in your belly to America.

Dayao didn't have money, but his family did. As if it were a dream, as if it had been a parlor trick. Dayao often dreamt of counting money – he'd count and count, until he awoke in a fright. Every time he awoke he was happy, and exhausted, though when he thought back on it they seemed more like nightmares.

And now this. The damned lass thought her family was poor, an embarrassment to her. But what did she know? Did she know all of her life's secret twists and turns? Not by a long shot.

Han Yuejiao grieved with him. She hesitated: "Maybe . . . maybe tonight we should tell her that we're not a poor family after all."

"No," said Dayao. He was firm on this point. "Absolutely not. The get of the poor are great, the sons of the rich wastrels . . . You think I don't know her? The moment we tell her she'll drop the ball. If she doesn't work hard, she'll never amount to squat."

But the more Dayao thought the angrier he got, and the angrier he got the more bitter he felt. He shouted in the direction of his long-vanished daughter: "I've got money! Your old da is rolling in it!"

He'd finally said it. That felt good. That was more like it.

A young man passing by laughed. He inclined his head and said, "I heard every word!"

## 4

This Michelle really was something – it was just an hour of English practice, but she insisted on doing it on a soccer field. Wasn't she worried about the sun on such a hot day? The lass usually hated being out in the sun, but as her face hardened she insisted on going to the pitch. She was being stubborn; she was still trying to gall her parents. Fine, then – go if you want to go. Anyway, the atmosphere at home was heavy and uncomfortable. So long as you're diligent, you're learning no matter where you are, right?

The sun glared overhead, and there was no one besides Michelle and Yao Zihan on the pitch. They weren't far from home, but Yao Zihan had never been in a place like this. She was frightened by its emptiness – or rather by its size. And also by its garishness: the grass was an expanse of emerald green, surrounded by a brick-red running track, which was itself divided by white lines that zipped all the way down to the end. The stands were even more riotous: painted a different color for each zone. Majestic. Brilliant. Grand. Yao Zihan surveyed her surroundings, feeling a little dizzy – it must have been particularly warm on the soccer field. Michelle told her that back in Michigan she'd been a "very good" soccer player, and had even made the papers. She liked soccer, this "girl's sport." Yao Zihan didn't understand how soccer could be a "girl's sport." Of course it is, Michelle explained. Men only like American football. She didn't like it at all, it was "too brutal."

As they conversed – that is to say, as they held class – they didn't notice that the sun had grown milder. The storm clouds were gathering overhead – it was too late, entirely too late. The clouds were gathering with greedy speed, and would break at any instant. As Yao Zihan realized what was happening she covered her head, and watched as Michelle opened her arms and leaned her head back, opening her mouth to the Heavens. Now that was a mouth worthy of the name. It was at once alarming and alluring. The raindrops struck her face and bounced off, leaping and dancing. Michelle went crazy, and yelled at the top of her voice: "Here . . . comes . . . the . . . love!" By the time her voice faded she was thoroughly soaked, her alarming breasts swelling through her shirt.

"Here comes the love?" A crazy thing to say – before Yao Zihan had time to ask, Michelle had grabbed hold of her and taken off running. It was a deluge, so heavy the ground smoked. After Yao Zihan had taken seven or eight steps some mysterious inner part of her body came to life, and her spirit awoke. If she hadn't been in the midst of it, Yao Zihan would never have experienced the sweet pleasure of a hard rain. It was new and strange kind of physical contact, like a secret not yet revealed, tempting yet troubling.

The rain was too much. In just a few minutes there was standing water on the green. Michelle let go of Yao Zihan's hand and took off towards one of the goals. As she turned and came back, she acted as if she'd just made a goal. Her face was exultant, and her finishing move was a long slide across the grass, on her knees. She took it a little too far, and nearly crashed into Yao Zihan. Even after her body had come to rest, her breasts seemed to continue their struggle. "Goal!!" she shouted. "*Goal*!!" With hardly a pause, she shouted: "Why aren't you celebrating?"

Of course she would celebrate. Yao Zihan dropped to her knees, raising a splash. The two teammates embraced ecstatically, overflowing with ecstacy, as if they really had just won the World Cup. What a thrill! How fucking awesome! It had all popped out of nowhere, as real as anything.

The rain fell harder, and Yao Zihan erupted with a desire to scream out loud. Michelle had been teaching her quite a bit of what they called special vocabulary, and without giving it a thought she shouted something dirty in English: "You're a fucking slut!"

Michelle was soaked through, her face dripping, strands of hair running with raindrops. Through the thick-falling rain Yao Zihan could see the corners of her mouth spreading in opposite directions behind her messed-up hair. She was smiling, crookedly.

"I am," she said.

Rainwater flowed rapidly down Yao Zihan's face. She had frightened herself. There was no way she could have said something like that in Chinese. Foreign languages were strange – you could say anything you liked – but now the "translation" was ringing in her head, disturbing her. What had she said! Perhaps seeking some balance, she squeezed her fists tight, lifted her head, and shouted at the sky:

"I'm a fucking slut, too!"

They both started laughing, and could not stop. The rain roared down, and the two young women roared with laughter until they were dizzy. But then the rain stopped, with no warning, much as it had started. Yao Zihan desperately wished the rain would keep falling – would fall forever. But it stopped, it disappeared, and left Yao Zihan soaked and exposed on the soccer field. The field was washed clean, and all its colors appeared in their original form: the green brilliant, the red bloody, the white snowy, all shockingly unreal.

## 5

The fainting spell came over Yao Zihan while she was practicing *guzheng*. It was startling. She collapsed over the instrument with a twanging bang, snapping several of the strings. What could have made her faint? It was just a cold; she'd been taking cold medicine for a couple of days. Han Yuejiao bitterly regretted letting her daughter out the door when she had a fever. On the other hand, this wasn't the first time. When had she ever let a headache or a fever stop her? She refused to miss a single class. "The others are making progress!" That's what she always said, usually stamping a foot. It's what Han Yuejiao found most lovable about the girl, and of course also what made her most proud.

When Dayao and Han Yuejiao rushed in they found Yao Zihan half-conscious. She'd vomited, and her front was covered in partially-digested dinner. Dayao had never seen his darling in this state. He gave a cry, and started weeping. Rather than panicking, Han Yuejiao set about cleaning her daughter up. No one knows a girl like her mother. She knew that Yao Zihan would hate being so filthy, so she made it look like it didn't happen. If Zihan knew, she might go silent for three or four days, at least.

Clearly, it was more than a cold. Yao Zihan had been a sickly child, and Han Yuejiao was no stranger to hospitals – she knew her way around blood tests, temperatures, medicines, and IV drips. But this time was completely different. The nurses wouldn't say anything. The tests they were running didn't appear to be regular blood tests, either. The needle was alarmingly long, around ten centimeters. Dayao and Han Yuejiao watched from behind glass as the nurses turned Yao Zihan over, opened her dress, and exposed her lower back. The nurse held the long needle over the middle of her back, and plunged it in. What was drawn out was not blood, but what looked like water. It seemed to be thirty or forty ccs of water. Dayao and Han Yuejiao were beside themselves with worry; sensing the gravity of the situation from the number of unfamiliar tests. Two hours later, the situation's gravity was confirmed by medical instruments. Tests of her spinal fluid came back with a protein level of 890, far in excess of the normal level of around 450. Her white blood cell count was a shocking 560, fifty-six times the normal amount. The doctor relayed the clinical significance of these figures to Dayao: "Inflammation of the brain parenchyma. Brain fever." Daoyao didn't know what parenchyma was, but he understood "brain fever," and he sat down heavily on the polished tile of the hospital floor.

## 6

Yao Zihan finally awoke from her coma a week later. It had been an experience worse than death for Dayao and Han Yuejiao. They had kept a silent watch by her bedside, gazing at one another in moments of despair. They were furtive, dread-filled, helpless looks, looks of inexpressible pain. The glances were brief, the pain they saw in each other's eyes unbearable. They watched as their eyes sunk, and darkened. Unaccustomed to embracing, they nevertheless held each other up and leaned against the other in the hospital. Otherwise neither could have stayed upright. There was hope in their hearts, but as time crept slowly on, hope receded. They had no desire but that their daughter might one day open her eyes again, and speak. If only she could speak again, they would gladly give their lives – even if it meant she would be sent to an orphanage, they would be happy.

Michelle was dutiful – she'd called Dayao from the gate of their building. As soon as he heard her voice anger swept over him. If she hadn't insisted on Zihan going to the soccer field, the lass wouldn't have gotten this ghastly illness. He had no real right to push all blame on to her, though. He was a plumber at a teachers college, after all. "Please don't call again," he managed to say with great restraint and courtesy. After hanging up, he paused, then deleted her number for good measure.

Hope can never be bought with human suffering, but heaven did finally smile upon them. On the morning of the eighth day – dawn, to be precise – Yao Zihan finally opened her eyes. It was Han Yuejiao who noticed first. She was in shock, and her scalp tingled. But she didn't cry out. She didn't dare feel happy. She simply looked at Zihan with complete focus. She was looking, studying her expression. Great heaven above, a smile crept onto her face. She was smiling at Han Yuejiao, her eyes limpid and lively, her gaze in silent communion with her mother's.

Yao Zihan looked at her mother, and her lips parted weakly. she said, "ma." Han Yuejiao could hear no sound, but she could tell by the shape of Zihan's mouth that she was calling for her mother, calling out – it was true. Han Yuejiao's answer welled up from the depths of her heart. She kept answering, she needed to grab hold. Dayao, sensing something, followed her into the room. Yao Zihan's limpid gaze shifted from her mother's face to her father's. She was smiling, only a little wearily. This time she spoke audibly.

"Dad," she said in English.

"What?" he asked.

"Where is this place?"

Dayao stared at her, uncomprehending, then leaned in closer and asked, "What are you saying?"

"Please tell me, what happened? Why aren't I at home? God, why are you two so thin? Have you been pushing yourselves too hard? Mom, if you don't mind, would you tell me if you two are sick?"

Dayao stared fixedly at his daughter. She seemed perfectly normal, apart from being tired – but what on earth was she saying? Why couldn't she speak Chinese? "Lass," he said. "Speak sense."

"Thank you, boss. Thank you very much for giving me such a respectable job, and of course such a respectable salary. I could never have afforded a piano otherwise. I have to say I still think it's too expensive, but I like it."

"Lass, it's your father. Speak properly!" Dayao was seeing double, he couldn't hold himself together. "Doctor!" he shouted, in a near-squeak.

"And my thanks to all the judges, thank you very much. I'm very happy to be here. May I have a glass of water? It seems I'm not expressing myself clearly, allow me to repeat myself: May I have a glass of water? Water. God . . . "

Dayao reached out his hand, and covered his daughter's mouth. He couldn't understand her, but he couldn't bear to hear any more. He was terrified, dread-filled. Hurried footsteps sounded in the corridor, and Dayao stripped off his shirt. He knew for sure his daughter needed emergency assistance, she needed a transfusion. He was willing to open every vein in his body; he was willing to give until he was dry as a bone.

*Translated by Eric Abrahamsen*

王安忆

# Wang Anyi

Wang Anyi was born in Nanjing. In 1980 she attended the Chinese Writers' Association Literature Academy and in 1983 participated in the Iowa University's International Writing Program. In 1987 she became a writer at the Shanghai Writers' Association and in 2004 took a professorship in Chinese at Fudan University. She has published the novels *Song of Everlasting Sorrow*, *Age of Enlightenment*, *Scent of Heaven*, *Bao Town*, *San Lian*, *Uncle's Story* and *Tian Xian Pei*. She has won the National Short Story Prize, the Mao Dun Literature Prize, the Lu Xun Literature Prize, the *China Times* "Kai Juan" Book Prize, and Malaysia's First World Chinese Literature "Hua Zong" Prize. Her works have been translated into English, German, Dutch, French, Russian, Italian, Spanish, Japanese, Hebrew, Korean, and Vietnamese.

# 云低处

# In the Belly of the Fog

## By Wang Anyi

That this particular couple should appear on this particular overnight train seems unnatural.

Most of the passengers on this local train over the plains of the northern border are farmers. They all wear winter clothes of dusted blue or black, while at their feet lie satchels of the same color and over-stuffed shape. Occasionally, a flame of brightness flickers between them, the peach-pink or blue-green of a woman's ski jacket, the gold hoops at her ears. Yet the color is a bit offensive, and does nothing but make the ambiance of gray depression all the more disappointing. Outside is only pure black – probably ten or eleven o'clock at night. Human shadows flicker to and fro over the double-paned windows, followed by threads of tiny lights that run across the glass like hairline cracks, then vanish instantly. When the train arrives at a station, the windows all light up, admitting the shadows of those without. Yet the light dispersed into the train car washes out the view of things inside. The recycled air from the heaters, the moisture of human breath and the miasma of tobacco collect into one clearly visible gaseous entity that oozes between bodies. Then the train leaves the station, the light on the windows fades and dies out, and all returns to shadow. The scenery inside the car condenses and turns in on itself. There is one instant when everything stands out, outlines become sharp, yet it all falls back into void moments later. But the train moves so slowly and stops so frequently that soon enough this brief instant of clarity loses its ability to attract attention. So even this subtle transformation sinks out of sight, and time and the trip stretch out into a single line in the darkness.

Of course, even a local night train like this one has a soft sleeper carriage! Passengers come and go so frequently here that the door to the car is always open, and the light always on – though, perhaps because of a scant current or a bad battery, it shines only weakly. The soft-sleeper passengers are hardly peasants, yet they also wear heavy, dark clothing against the northern winter. Their eyelids are swollen, presumably from lack of sleep, blurring the contours of their North Asiatic features. The dusky lamp above throws down shadows of all sizes and shapes, and people sit submerged in shadows, each husbanding untrustworthy motives and expressions. The tracks are quite old, and the train wobbles heavily. At every switch in the rails it slams loudly, followed by a full-body shiver, as if the old train were gritting its teeth and jumping right over. Followed by more wobbling. The soft-sleeper compartment wall blocks the light from outside, so the scenery inside doesn't change when the train nears a station. Even as passengers go out and come in, it can be hard to tell the difference; new people and empty beds are all hidden in darkness. Mid-winter. North China. The same people, the same winter clothes, the same North Asiatic faces.

The man and woman get on the train separately. When the man enters the soft-sleeper car, the woman is lying on her bunk. Light from the station shines into their compartment. On the floor, which has lost its paint to years of salt water and will never be clean again if the stains go any deeper, sits a low-cut deerskin boot. The material has turned gray-black, with a few patches of the original yellow still vaguely visible. The boot's collapsing top with its soft wrinkles identifies it as real deerskin. From one angle, one can even see the embroidered flower pattern at the top. The other boot is lost in a shadow somewhere. The train stands a while at the platform, then pulls away. This boot is also lost to the darkness, becoming a formless pile of shadow. The man judges that the owner of the boot is a woman, and certainly not from anywhere along this line. The woman wakes up on her bunk. Her lazy consciousness is being invaded by a voice speaking in a crisp Beijing accent. This accent rings strongly in the throat, and it sounds sharp, even a little cold, compared to the heavy northwestern accents around it. This voice hops and flows around the compartment with unnatural vivacity, stirring up the dull miasma of heavier sounds. It brightens up the leaden space, as if carrying its light with it. She determines that it is a new voice. It breaks through the utterly unexceptional surroundings, and brings the wide outside world in along with it. Yet by doing so it only makes this little world seem more remote, as if it has gone on its solitary route and been forgotten. She turns her face from the wall toward the interior of the compartment. The voice is coming from the corridor beyond. It sounds cheerful, which already seems out of place in this environment. Soon after, a figure is silhouetted in the doorway. This figure not only does not adumbrate the inside of the compartment, it actually intensifies the light that slips around it from the corridor. Apparently, that space is quite bright. She feels the owner of the voice has arrived. His shadow, like his voice, cuts a clear outline of itself amid a hazy atmosphere. He leaps through the door, and leaps again over to the bunk opposite her, where he sits down. The two outsiders are now face-to-face.

Her body and her face are in shadow, but this sets off the brightness of her eyes. They sparkle with a quiet light. Not slept in three days, have you? he asks her with a smile. The grey background makes his skin appear particularly white. His face is one of the handsome types one finds in the north: long, with single eyelids, long-tailed eyes, a straight nose, and thin lips. The legendary Pan An, Adonis of ancient times, probably had a face like his. His height is obvious even when he's sitting down, as his two long legs occupy the space between the bunks. His shoulders are broad and flat, his waist narrow – very well-shaped. He rests his elbows on his knees and stares at the eye gleaming at him from the shadow opposite. He has no way to guess her age, yet this eye is enough to give him a fairly clear impression. He knows this must be the owner of the deerskin boots. The train has just made another stop, and now sets off again. Station lights pass the windows one by one, and the deerskin boot on the floor comes in and out of view, its top still softly crumpled. When he first asked her this facetious question, she had begun to respond, yet swallowed it at the last minute. She is clearly not in the mood to laugh. Her face turns back to the wall. With her form overshadowed by the upper bunk, he can't tell if she's lying on her side or on her back. But

Illustration by Tan Tan

as soon as her eyes disappear from view, the rest of her seems to retreat completely into nothingness.

An unknown amount of time passes; slow trains always have that effect. Rolling over this desolate northern territory, they seem quite isolated from the world. The small stations where they stop are all cold and quiet, with no feeling of life to them. A few sounds from beyond the window: running footsteps, the peal of a whistle, an exchanged word or two. Just a few needlepoint-sized atoms that come from the freezing emptiness and ping once or twice before they disappear.

When she turns back over, the opposite bunk is empty, yet a hand-held video game player on the tea table before the window signifies that he hasn't left yet. That crisp Beijing accent is silent, yet the air is still excited, so he must still be on the train. Sure enough, he comes back not long afterwards. When he arrives, he finds her sitting up on her bunk, playing with his handset. The game is Tetris, and the battery must be low because the images on the screen are very faint, and she has to hold it at a certain angle to make out the little block figures raining down from above. She's really into the game, and holds the screen almost up to her nose in order to see clearly. Her face and hair are half-hidden behind the stand-up collar of her down jacket. The jacket looks like a man's, both heavy and baggy. It makes her look young. He knows she isn't that young – why? No reason. He just has that feeling. Of course, she isn't old yet, either – also a feeling. The truth is, he can't even see her face clearly, he just senses she is in her richest years of experience and emotion. He sits on the low bunk opposite her and watches her play. They both sense that, on some level, they are of the same kind. Part of that is the environment, which has forced both of them out into the open. He watches her play for a while, then says, Don't stare at the screen so hard, it isn't good for you. His tone carries a note of concern – concern which, on this dark journey, suggests a certain vulnerability.

She takes his advice, holding the handset farther away and adjusting to a more comfortable position before starting up another game. Now, they've made a connection, and they can talk to each other. He does most of the talking. What is she traveling for? he asks. Is she selling a product . . . or collecting debt, maybe? She looks up at him sharply and shakes her head. From this, one could conclude she is not very well-acquainted with the world, and maybe even an introvert. Well then, how did she end up on a provincial train like this one? Now he's curious. He starts asking about her profession. She doesn't tell him, so he guesses: project assistant? Newspaper reporter? Actress, even? She answers neither yes nor no, but it's clear she is in a better mood now than she had been. She turns to face him. Her features cut the downward-shining lamplight into distinct shapes of light and shadow, giving her face a three-dimensional feel. He considers the face for a moment, then says: You look like you're in economics. This actually makes her smile – only for a second, though, and she pulls it back in immediately as if she had some powerful reason not to smile. Yet she puts down the handset and looks straight at him. She finds his way of speaking entertaining. The train is stopping again; this station is even more desolate, probably because of the hour, which is already past twelve. Light from the station passes through the window and shines on her face. The change is significant: now it looks wide and flat, yet with a healthful glow. Then the train starts off again, the light fades, and she recovers her previous appearance. He's sitting at an angle, his back to the door, so the change in light doesn't affect him. Besides, with sharp features like his, his face is always the same set, definite representation; he is always attractive. This is another reason she enjoys listening to him.

He starts talking about himself. He's done everything: real estate, futures, selling official permissions, producing shows. He knows a number of celebrities, and lists off a whole slew of them in one breath: so-and-so, so-and-so, so-and-so, along with so-and-so's son, daughter, mistress. His grandiloquence is suspicious, especially on a backwoods train like this one. What would a high-flyer like himself be doing here? Most of the passengers here are peasants or small-time businessmen. They get off at some tiny, no-name station, carrying their bundles of clothing, toiletries, machine parts, or expired medicines, and disappear into the nameless corridors of night. Yet he scoots closer to the window and, looking at the glass, says, I have so much money, I could raise a whole harem if I felt like it. This boast doesn't come off as self-satisfied, but is mixed instead with a note of sadness. She detects this, and asks, Are you happy? Not at all, is the definite answer. Now he sounds believable. Of course, everything on this local overnight train is tinged with melancholy.

No sound comes from the bunks above, though both are occupied. Are the passengers asleep, or are they listening? They're quiet, at any rate. The other passengers seem to have acknowledged these two are of their own kind and not of theirs. That they should be talking to each other is perfectly natural. Still, no reason why they can't listen in! Thus, even the shadows have eyes and can hear plainly. Occasionally, other people go by in the corridor. Time blurs during a trip like this – maybe they think it's still day! Yet the presence of night is still detectable in the stupid woodenness of passengers' movements. While his Beijing accent is clear, cool, and sharp, and slices right through the heavy air of the train. Their faces, especially his, carry a certain sharpness that cuts open time. While hers, being more three-dimensional, opens in a way that isn't so eye-catching, yet has more depth to it. The atmosphere of this car in this compartment is changed, the airflow altered. Here, the quiet night is a little more restless.

Each asks where the other is getting off – both at the same place, a major station ahead. The great majority of passengers will be getting off there, and many other people will get on. The station lies right at the border of two provinces. Its name is grand and familiar, and hearing it gives one a feeling like a hole has opened in the void through which one can escape. Hope flashes in the heart. He asks her what she'll be doing there; she still doesn't reply. Nor does he dwell on it. A woman from the outside world, who looks like she's "in economics," riding a provincial non-express train at night – what could she be doing? Still, in a world where truth is stranger than fiction, anything can happen! He tells her what he's here for without waiting for her to ask. He is indisputably the talkative one, and if it weren't for that crisp Beijing accent, it would be too much. He seems to be intent on using conversation to break the pressure of the night. He says he's arranged with a couple of Hong Kong businessmen to meet in that inter-provincial coastal city, from which they'll set off for some island with a forgettable name. They're going to check out the local economy; the island is known for producing apples, along with a variety of seafood products, and it's becoming a hot target for development. He looks over at her. Her face is once again enveloped in shadow, only the outline of one cheek visible as a lighter patch on a dark background. The train shudders hard; then, a loud clang as it jumps a switch. A glint on the outline of her cheek – something is sparkling. He feels that she is crying. Not that there is anything strange about that; it's perfectly natural. Moreover, her crying is even a little easier to bear than her not, as if it were softening a sharp edge. He too feels a twinge in his nose. Even though neither of them knows anything about the other; they are still strangers.

He becomes gentler. Gentleness is incompatible with his handsome face. The over-adored features reveal traces of old wounds as they assume an expression of sympathy. He moves farther over to one side of the tea table to face her directly; now he, too, is half-covered in shadow. He says, You know, we have an extra space in the car. Come with us. No, she replies. She says so little, he can get no clear impression of her voice or accent. At the very least it doesn't have the glottal harshness belonging to natives of these parts. The two of them already understand that, even as compatriots on this local night train, the distance between them is still very great – too great even for words of comfort.

The door at the front of the car slams open, and there is the sound of leather shoes. It's the midnight police patrol. They tramp down the corridor and throw open the door at the other end. When that slams shut it coincides with another hard track change, which resounds like a disproportionately loud echo. The darkness inside the car oozes like an object with physical density, slowly covering everything over, yet when it gets to these two, it goes around them, as if forced away by some magnetic anti-polarity. It's very obvious they are both creatures from the outside world. That world is vigilant, with hard, sharp thorns that stick out and interweave, and train them to be alert, nervous, shrewd. Their forms are brighter, the material of their bodies more tightly meshed, and therefore liable to stand out in this lightless, unforming space.

Another stop. Light from the station lamps filters through the double-paned window and falls on her booted foot. The deerskin boot softly covers her foot. A wave of wrinkles by the heel communicates the clever knit of her bones. It's the heel of a creature from the outside world that's already stepped over who knows how many different kinds of road. A person outside stops and looks in through the window. With his back to the light, his face is entirely black. The moment feels like a dream – human shadows moving like paper figurines. The figure stands a while, then moves off. The train waits a moment, then silently slips away itself. The faint noise of a whistle reaches them, as if it had carried over far mountain ranges. He looks at his watch, says, We're almost there.

The train has moved onto an inter-provincial track. It picks up speed, and its rhythm over the tracks becomes clear and regular. Inside the car, the borders of light and darkness become more distinct, outlines more definite. This leg of the journey seems to drag out for two or three times the length of the previous leg, and the travel becomes smoother. The atmosphere of accumulated anxiety seems a little lighter. They both collect their luggage and go to stand in the vestibule by the exit doors. The light there is much better. Each examines the other, discovers things that were different moments ago in the dark. It's as if they both have lost a little color – not gotten darker, but paler, more diluted. Yet, no matter what, each already has an impression of the other, and new alterations do nothing to change the original image. In fact, being exposed like this under normal light makes them seem more easily understandable to each other. He looks at her, and says again: You really do look like you're in economics. Is this praise? Or is he trying to get her to be closer to him, to make her someone he can better understand? She smiles, although that doesn't alleviate her worried look, but only makes it more sorrowful. Yet, seen under full-on light, her sorrow is more fully revealed, and seems closer to the surface and more understandable. He earnestly entreats her – this earnestness distorts his overly-symmetrical face, making it ugly, yet honest. He entreats her, Come with us. He trusts she is moved, because she turns her face away, and emphatically replies, No. His face relaxes with the recognition of final defeat. He lets out a small sigh, then, as if by way of compromise, asks, Is someone picking you up? She gives him no answer.

The grind of train wheels on steel track grows louder. The engine shrugs off the lethargy of a local train and starts to run freely, imparting a sense of the strength of its speed. This strength breaks through the crust of the night and opens a snow-white tunnel. Up ahead is a major station; on the platform, a line of brilliant lights stands at attention. The train passes under a footbridge, rattling the bridge's underpinnings with the echoing rip of its whistle, and pulls into the station in a blast of baptismal energy. They debark one after another. Under the black sky, the platform lights seem to lean together into a vaulted arch leading toward an opening above their heads. They walk into that opening, and gradually separate.

*Translated by Canaan Morse*

叶弥

# Ye Mi

Born in Suzhou in 1964, Ye Mi was six years old when her parents were sent down to the countryside. She first started writing fiction in 1994. Ye Mi received the Lun Xun Literature Prize for her short story "Incense Burner Mountain"; Jiang Wen's 2007 film *The Sun Also Rises* was loosely based on "Velvet".

# 月亮的温泉

# The Hot Springs on Moon Mountain

## By Ye Mi

G u Qingfeng tended three and a half acres of Mexican marigolds that were her heart and soul. They filled the flower beds before and behind her house, on the banks of the creek on the west side, and on the southward face of the hill by the creek. Mexican marigolds come in gold, sunfire red, and tangerine. She liked tangerine the best, so that was all she grew. There was a reason for it: the first time she met her husband, he was coming toward her over the wooden bridge at the head of the village as the sun rose behind him in an orange glow. A sea of tangerine orange light buoyed him up with the sun and pervaded his whole form. Even today, the image made her feel safe and happy.

Her marigolds were by far the brightest of any that grew in the area. Local women whispered that she could communicate with them. At some point, people just started calling her Marigold. They used it so often, her husband joined in. When local cadres brought guests around to show off her land, they would sometimes say her name was Mary – Mary Gold.

Every day she rose before dawn, made congee for the family, then went up the hill to cut grass for the pig. When the sun rose, she gave herself to her three and a half acres of marigolds. Her husband was a handsome man who could play the flute and the *er'hu*, and had a lovely singing voice. But he liked food and clothes, and didn't care for farm work. After breakfast, he'd go for a walk, whistling as he went. People out in the fields would hear the whistle and say, "Shame! Marigold's home alone again."

Her whistling man often ate lunch away from the house, but would often come home for a nap before going out again. Sometimes he wouldn't come back until the evening. The villagers joked that he was a duck she raised with the other animals.

But Marigold had other ideas. Her favorite part of every long, tiring day was after he'd finished dinner and would say, "Marigold, do you want me to massage your back?" or "Come here, Marigold, let me rub your shoulders." She would usually reply, "It's fine, I'm not tired. Why don't you go lie down?" Marigold didn't like to talk, and on your average day wouldn't say more than a few sentences. Her husband would say that her mouth was only good for eating, and that she was the most standoffish woman in the whole village.

And who was the most engaging?

The most engaging woman in the village was Fang. Two years ago, someone had discovered hot springs on Moon Mountain that were purportedly full of essential minerals. Bathing in them frequently was guaranteed to revitalize the body and prolong life. And who wouldn't want that? So someone immediately built a spa resort on the mountain called The Lunar Palace; soon, men and women were swarming in from the outside like hungry ants. They stripped off their colorful clothes and steeped themselves in the steaming water, their eyes half-closed, as if their souls were evaporating too.

The Lunar Palace was hidden deep amid the mountains and surrounded by the pillared trunks of ancient trees. Droves of young women came from within and outside the mountains, and put down roots there just like the trees had. Fang was the first from their village to go. When she came back two months later to see her family, she was wearing bright red lipstick and clothes the local girls would never forget. Now, they all understood that Fang's mouth had several uses: it could say captivating things, eat expensive food, and decorate itself with different colors of lipstick. As she talked, she pulled five or six tubes out of her purse and turned them up to show everyone.

"See, this one's pink, this one's plum, this one's tangerine…"

"But why would you wear it?"

"Idiot, men like it! When they kiss you, they'll think of Elizabeth Taylor's lips."

"Well, who's Elizabeth Taylor?"

"Idiot, you don't even know her? If you want to make money, if you want to really know things, get yourself to the hot springs!"

Fang had one of the girls take the tangerine lipstick to Marigold. Fang said to the girl, "You remind her that she was once the prettiest, classiest girl in the village. I'm sure she knows whether she has the kind of life she deserves. If she calls me names, I'll just laugh. If she throws the lipstick away, I'll just feel sorry for her."

After the lipstick made it to Marigold, she cursed Fang up and down and threw the tube in the pigsty without even looking at it. Her mood was foul all day, and she could almost hear Fang giggling and sighing in her ear. Unable to focus, she put down her farm work and waited by the road for her husband.

It was already getting dark by the time her husband appeared, gliding along perfectly at ease like a wandering hermit. "What... exactly do you do all day?" Marigold timidly asked.

He raised his eyebrows and stiffened his neck. "What do you mean by that?"

Marigold didn't want to cause tension, and so she laughed, "Oh, nothing! I just missed you a lot today!"

Her husband relaxed and said, "Actually, to tell you the truth, *I* don't even know what I do all day."

"Then why do you like to be away all the time?"

"Because it's better than being at home," he replied with conviction. "All the women in our village are gone except for the girls and the grandmas. Who could bear staying at home at a time like this?"

He yawned several times as he spoke.

There sure were a lot of people who liked the outside world. Ever since Fang came back to visit, the other young women in the village screwed up their courage and ran off to Moon Mountain. Marigold was the only woman of her age left. Only she still lived her life the way she always had, watching over her fields of flowers.

Fang stayed at the resort for a year, then came back again, this time only for a day. Once again, she had remade herself. She looked like aristocracy, arriving in a sparkling yellow dress, and leaving in a bright red Western business suit. Even though she only stayed the day, what a day it was. She laid out plans to turn her parents' house into a gaming parlor, help her older brother's family open a cinema, and have her younger brother start a hair salon. And after she left, her family made it happen. From then on, the clatter of mah-jongg tiles continued day and night; the young boys and girls stopped singing songs and flirting in the outdoors, and went to grope each other in the dark theater. A pair of young ladies from away came to work at the salon. They said they weren't used to the heat and humidity here, so they wore blouses with low necklines and miniskirts, and sat with their legs crossed in front of the shop window, cigarettes in hand. The village boys couldn't think of anything else.

But this is all epilogue.

The evening Fang left, Marigold's husband came home looking unhappy. "I saw Fang," he said. "She was riding in a car. She kept waving at me, like she was mayor or something. I remember back when all she could do was talk; she had nothing on you. Look at the class she's got now! She stopped the car and asked me how you'd been. How the hell do you think…I turned around and walked off. What could I say? Look at you now – you can't even compare to what you used to be, let alone to her. You don't care for yourself, and you certainly don't care about me."

Marigold sat dumbstruck for a moment, then asked plaintively, "How have I not cared about you?"

"You can't even figure that out?" her husband shot back. "You've seen Fang's family, walking around with their noses in the air."

"Let's talk about this later," said Marigold in a placating tone. "Massage my shoulder, it's really sore."

Her husband, clearly not finished, stood with his hands at his sides and glared at her.

Marigold grabbed her husband's wrist and pummeled her shoulder with it. His hand was a cold, dead weight that only moved where she moved it. The minute she relaxed her grip, it disappeared. She felt a soreness spread throughout her whole body, reaching deep into her bones, so painful it made her eyes start with tears.

The two of them ate a flavorless dinner. Before the light failed she said to her husband, "Come on, let's go look at the marigolds."

They went around to the back of the house. The sun was setting into a valley in the west, and long spears of orange light fell over the marigold beds, making the flowers look even softer. Marigold felt a pang in her heart, and started to cry again.

"Again with the crying?" Her husband was annoyed. "Twice in just a couple of hours, it's not like anybody's died."

Marigold dried her eyes and said, "I was just thinking of that time I first saw you on the bridge."

Her husband looked at her intently for a moment, then sat down on the mud wall of the field and said in a softer tone, "Forgive me for being so harsh with you. I was only twenty-one then. That day I was eating a bowl of corn congee, and just as I was finishing I heard two other guys from our village talking about you on the other side of the wall. They said you were the prettiest girl around. I couldn't resist going to look for you. I never expected I'd run into you right there on the bridge... You were so much prettier than Fang back then. Who was she? Just some crazy, dark-skinned girl with no meat on her bones. What gives her the right to be on top?"

"I didn't see her either of the times she came back," Marigold muttered. "I can't imagine how pretty she is now. Are the hot springs really that nice, that they can turn a sparrow into a phoenix?"

A cold gust of wind blew over them, and her husband huddled his shoulders together. The sun lost its footing and slipped beneath the valley. Mountains, trees, wind, and clouds all became dark and heavy. Marigold didn't hear her husband's answer to her question, so she changed topics and asked if Fang had said anything to him. Her man responded without a second thought: "She said the resort had everything a woman could want."

The next day, Marigold rose before dawn the way she always did. She cut grass for the pig, then came home to make congee for her family. After it was done, she went to check on her husband. He was awake, and lay wrapped up in the comforter, absorbed in his own thoughts. Marigold stood in front of him and said, "I'm going to the resort on Moon Mountain today. I'm going to see what's really up there."

Her husband turned over and said to the wall: "Go wherever you want. No need to tell me. I don't understand. It's none of my business. I didn't hear... Send the pig and the kid away when you go. I'm not dealing with them when you're not here."

Marigold tiptoed out of her husband's room and went to the marigold fields, where she worked as hard as she could until sunrise. When she came back, her husband was gone, having left his empty bowl on the table. Their son, whom they called Tree, was scratching lines in the floor. She washed his hands and made him eat a few mouthfuls of congee. Then she did the dishes, filled the wood box, put on clean clothes, and packed a bag with another change of clothing and two bags of dried marigold flowers.

With Tree beside her, she let the pig out and prepared to drop them both off at Auntie Ma's. As she walked, she looked everywhere around her, hoping to catch sight of her husband. Sadly, all she saw were memories: the broken wall where the two of them had hidden as young lovers, the tree they had leaned against as they sang to each other, the dyke where he had first kissed her… and the wooden bridge where they'd first fallen in love, one of them over here, the other over there.

Marigold finally realized that she wouldn't see her husband before she left. If he were intentionally hiding from her, he wouldn't hang around the village.

Marigold delivered her pig and her son to Auntie Ma. She told Auntie she was going to the resort – it was nothing important, she just wanted to see Fang and talk to her about something. Auntie Ma smacked her lips and said disapprovingly, "Go if you want to, I wasn't asking. Everybody says it's a nice place! They have lights on everywhere at night, and it's so bright you could see a hair on the ground. It's too bad I'm so old, and can't travel that far. Fang certainly is talented. She holds up half the sky for all the other women in this village!"

Auntie Ma stood on her doorstep, one hand shading her eyes, and watched Marigold until she disappeared. "All the girls in our village are

Illustration by Guo Xun

gone," she said ruefully. "Where? To the hot springs. To make money. To sell themselves."

Marigold crossed the wooden bridge. The water below her rushed and boiled with white foam. This scene had remained unchanged for centuries, and seemed as if it would stay that way. But the people were not what they were. She would carry her resentment all the way to Fang, and ask her why everything in the village changed after she came back. Even Marigold's husband lost his smile and didn't want to rub her back anymore. If her man didn't want to rub her back, then she obviously wasn't living the life she wanted. Fang was a smart woman; she need only look at Marigold's man to know the kind of life Marigold was living.

She walked along the road through the mountains from morning until sundown, with still no sign of the resort. She left the roadside for a small stream that ran close by, and sat down to eat the crackers she'd brought. Night had almost fallen, and a gusting wind shook the bamboo trees like a hail of arrows. It tore right through her, filling her ears with its howling voice.

Marigold threw away the crackers, buried her head in her knees and started to wail. She missed her son, missed the pig, missed her field of marigolds, and missed her husband the most. Everyone said he was lazy, and he was, sort of; but he was also sweet and considerate, happy and humming a tune all the time. Every time he saw her, his face would light up in a joyful smile. All Marigold needed was to see that smile, and she'd feel time reverse itself and take her back to their first meeting. Marigold wanted that smile more than all the riches there ever were.

Marigold was a rough, clumsy woman, but she couldn't go without love. Love made the sunlight warm and the flowers bright. It would let her live with energy and die without regret.

She cried for a while. When she raised her head, she found a man standing in front of her. She had no idea when he'd appeared there. He was covered in dust from the road, yet the gaze he fixed on her was focused and compassionate. He was clearly a man of solid temperament. Marigold connected with him immediately, as if they'd known each other for years already.

"Where are you headed, hon?" the man asked with a smile.

"I'm going to the hot springs on Moon Mountain," she said, wiping away tears. "Do you know how far they are?"

"I don't know how far they are," was the honest reply. "But I'm going there myself. I'm from Qinghe Village; my name is Miao Shanlin."

Marigold no longer felt like crying. "My name is Marigold," she said.

Miao Shanlin only had one hand. His whole arm was missing.

Now Marigold had a travel partner, and didn't need to fear the dark or being lonely. She walked as fast as she could, her pack over her shoulder; Miao Shanlin followed her, saying, "No need to run. If we take our time, we should get there in the evening, and that's when we want to be there. People say that the hot springs are a paradise at night, and they get busier as the night goes on. In the morning, everybody's asleep, and there isn't much going on." He pointed at the setting sun and asked, "Marigolds are that color, aren't they?"

Marigold smiled. "Pretty much."

"You're that color, too." Miao Shanlin continued.

Marigold pursed her lips in an embarrassed smile. "Pretty much." The things he said to her warmed her heart, and she walked even faster.

"What have you heard about the hot springs?" Miao Shanlin called out from behind her. The wind was at her back, and it carried his voice hurriedly past her and into the distance.

Marigold stopped to wait for him, and said, "I've heard that the hot springs are a young woman's paradise, that they have everything a young woman could want."

Miao Shanlin caught up to her, and said in a pressing tone, "I heard that the hot springs were a man's paradise, and that as soon as a man got there he would be dazzled, and forget his worries." They looked at each other for a moment, then fell silent.

The moon hadn't yet risen, and the night was completely black.

At one point as they walked, the road dove into a stand of trees, then turned down a bluff and into a valley in which points of light were scattered everywhere, like pearls.

That was the resort.

They stopped. The sudden transformation into brilliance made them afraid.

Marigold leaned against a boulder by the side of the road and took off her shoes; she had blisters on her feet. Miao Shanlin stripped the bark off a willow tree and told her to press it down over the blistered area as an analgesic. "My son's nickname is Tree," she said mournfully. "I've never left him before. I can't imagine how he must be crying tonight."

Miao Shanlin paused for a minute, then finally asked. "What about your husband?"

"My husband? My husband is a dreamer. He thinks all day about getting rich and living the good life. There's a girl in our village called Fang who came here to the hot springs and made lots of money. Now, when my husband thinks of her he can't stand me. Everything used to be great with us. He smiled every day. I miss his smile. Every time I saw it, I felt like life was good."

Marigold's voice got softer and softer. Soon she was crying, and had to dry her eyes on Miao Shanlin's empty sleeve. She only dabbed the sleeve over her eyes a few times before putting it down – it was inappropriate, after all. Then she asked him what happened to his arm.

Miao Shanlin turned to look out on the layers of mountains and black-patched forests, and told his story. He said that he once fell in love with a girl from his village. She loved him as well, so they got married and had a daughter. One day, a wealthy real estate developer who had dreams of turning their village into a resort community came to stay, and as he looked over the land he also looked over the women. In the end, he didn't find any real estate he liked, but he took a shine to Miao Shanlin's wife. The rest was predictable enough: the day the developer took her away, Miao Shanlin cut them off on the main road out of the village. The besotted woman took a knife and destroyed her husband's arm. After that, Miao Shanlin had one arm fewer than anyone else.

It was a long time before Miao Shanlin turned back around. He had been telling his story to the mountains and the trees, and crying as he did so.

He and a few others had worked hard selling herbal medicine, and he made some money. After hearing people say that a man with a troubled heart could go to the hot springs and heal all his wounds, he decided that was what he wanted to do most of all. He would find a gentle, pretty woman, spend all his money, and return home with a lighter step.

Now that the resort was right before his eyes, he no longer wanted to go. He felt afraid, though of what, he couldn't tell. He suddenly realized something: he missed women. He would find one, of course, but she had to be the kind of woman he liked. Marigold was that kind of woman. She had an air about her that was familiar and pleasing to him. His wife had had it when they were first married. It made him feel at peace, satisfied, and thankful; it inspired him to be closer to friends and family, and respectful to strangers. The herbal medicine business had taken him all over the country and shown him thousands of women. None of them possessed that same air – or, if they ever had, it was already gone. After he met Marigold, he felt it on her, and it reminded him of that idea he had once worshipped: that idea called "love." That reminder made him very happy.

Miao Shanlin kept talking to the mountains and trees.

"How about this: if you're not put off by me, you can have all the money I've got, if I can have you."

Miao Shanlin's offer was genuine, and Marigold took it seriously. Her brow furrowed, and she thought about it for a while. But she tossed away the willow bark in her hand, put on her shoes, stood up, and said one word to the back of Miao Shanlin's head: "No." She didn't explain why not, and Miao Shanlin didn't ask. He turned around; it was his turn to see the back of Marigold's head. "I'll wait for you here!" he called to her.

I'm going to the hot springs, Marigold said to herself, and she walked on. But suddenly she too felt uncertain – she didn't know what she was going to do there, either. She passed through the trees, turned, and crossed a stone bridge that put her on a broad avenue bordering the resort. There was a chill in the air. Cold ripples muttered in the river that ran alongside the avenue, and billows of white fog coursed down from the mountain to play in the streets before disappearing in the woods beyond the bridge. The avenue was full of shops, and the tables and chairs of food vendors were set up in a long line. Everything was illuminated by hot, brightly colored lights, which diluted the deep cold of the natural environment.

Marigold thought of Auntie Ma's description. The night here really was lit up as bright as day – you could drop a needle and find it with no problem. No wonder all the village girls came here. What did the village have? The sour odors of silage and livestock manure, and the smell of house mold on all of the people. Here, even the wind was fragrant with scents of fresh cooking oil, and ever-present traces of perfume. Marigold took it all in for a while, but didn't catch sight of anyone she knew.

Her stomach growled, reminding her she needed to eat something. Too tired to look around, she plopped herself down on the closest chair. The vendor was a solid-looking man in his early thirties, who came over and greeted her with: "What can I get you? We have beef stew and lamb stew, or would you like steamed partridge? The braised rabbit's good, too." Seeing that Marigold was in no mood to talk, he answered his own question: "How about a hot bowl of noodles with broth, then? You look like you need a big, steaming bowl of noodles with chili sauce."

The vendor had a perfectly round head with close-cropped hair, narrow, smiling eyes, and one sharp canine tooth that stuck out over his bottom lip. His smile reminded Marigold of her own husband, and made it hard for her to swallow her noodles. He was the gregarious type, and never stopped talking. "Eat, eat," he said. "The flour for the noodles comes from Sha'anxi, so they're really *al dente*. You don't look like you're here on vacation."

Marigold set down her bowl and quietly replied, "I'm looking for someone."

"Looking for who? I was one of the first vendors here, cross my heart, I know everyone in this town."

Just as he said this, someone seated in the adjoining stall snorted. "You, number one?" he asked. "If you're number one, who am I?"

"Of course I'm number one," affirmed the first vendor, patting his chest. "What the hell do I care who you are? Don't go looking for trouble. Listen, lady, forget about him, we'll figure this out. Who are you looking for?"

"I'm looking for Fang," was Marigold's response.

Hearing her answer, the vendor froze momentarily. His gaze changed, and he asked her intently, "How do you know Fang?"

Marigold, looking the vendor steadily in the eye, stuttered, "I'm family."

The vendor shook his head. "You don't look like family. You look like you're here looking for work. There's a lot of women who come around looking for Fang, because she knows how to talk, that's how she ended up the number one hooker in town. ("That's about right," muttered the person in the adjoining stall. "That's more like it.")

"She's eaten here several times. I even let her run a tab when she first came. In the end, she never paid it back, but she let me kiss her a few times behind the stall. That was her payment. Fine by me! She's the most capable woman in the whole resort – smart, pretty, and she's got money. She may not be educated, but she could beat any CEO for strategy and just getting things done. But she threw herself in the river today, jumped right off that bridge over there. It's sad..."

He pointed to the big stone bridge Marigold had crossed a few minutes before. As he turned back, his finger scraped across Marigold's cheek and made her twitch.

He wasn't done talking:

"The bottom there is all sharp rocks, and the water's freezing. The blood on the stones washed off immediately, as if nothing had ever happened... They sent her to the hospital, but if she's not dead she'll be paralyzed. If you want to go see her, I'll have my wife take you. The hospital's not far; if you take the road up the mountain, you should be there in twenty minutes or so."

The vendor ran off to find his wife as Marigold stood in shock. The person in the next booth leaned over and said, "Listen, honey, don't get yourself down. Something like this isn't really big news around here. If you work hard and learn to talk the way she could, you'll have a lot of money to send home too. Just don't let yourself get down the way she did. A person needs to look after number one. I look after myself. These last few nights I've been getting up too often to pee, and I started worrying..."

"Why would she kill herself?" Marigold mumbled.

"Possessed," said the other. "Otherwise, someone like her would never do it. Here, there are ghosts everywhere; they'll possess you if you're not careful. You know what 'substitute' means?" Marigold continued to stare into the distance and mumble to herself. "She was doing so well, why would she kill herself?"

The first vendor's wife crossed the street toward them, and her interlocutor turned away again, whispering, "I have no idea. I've wondered, too – with that kind of money and status, why would she kill herself? Obviously an idiot, at least not as clever as she looked." Then he started advertising to the crowd: "Live chicken live duck live fish silk-worms ants and graaaaaaaaass-hoppers! Put pep in your step, stay up all night!"

The vendor's wife had her hair in a perm, and her lips were bright red. She shuffled along in bathroom sandals and a pair of blue floral pants. She leaned slightly backward as she walked, so that one could see her breasts bob lazily back and forth beneath her blouse. Her husband had called her away from the mah-jongg table, and she was clearly indignant, glowering and muttering as she came, and examining Marigold with a dubious look. But she recognized the girl's provincial, timid demeanor, and this lightened her mood.

"Let's go!" she called. "So are you really from Fang's family?"

Marigold, walking dutifully behind her, responded in the affirmative. "Yes, I guess so."

"Not much of a talker, are you?"

"No." Another one-syllable answer.

The vendor's wife looked at her again, and said with a sweetened disdain, "My man says you want to work here, but you won't make it looking like that. How could you? You're sure not prettier than me; you couldn't even compete with somebody like Fang. And look what happened to her."

She stood up, lit a cigarette, and took a drag. Moonlight, which fell full on the pathway up the mountain, lit up the two women and threw their diminutive shadows onto the cobblestone. When the figures moved, their shadows shattered. The stones were wet; skeins of fog like strips of cloud snaked across the road in front of them.

"What did Fang really kill herself for?" Marigold asked. The vendor's wife pulled out another cigarette and passed it to her, saying, "Why'd she do it? I was thinking just that back at the mah-jongg table. My guess is she killed herself for a man. You see if I'm wrong. Think about it – besides that, what else does a woman have to worry about? Especially a woman like her." Marigold took the cigarette and started to smoke. The vendor's wife gave a short laugh, and said, "I know her. We were all birds who flew in from outside the mountains, then learned how to tempt men. But we didn't have the smarts, couldn't get ahead like she did. All we could do was use our art to find us a husband, then go back to the straight and narrow. I'm not trying to be mean, but even if you do want to work here, you don't have what it takes. Not unless you have some incredible luck."

Then the vendor's wife told her a story about luck. She said there was once a man out there who was so poor he couldn't afford a wife at forty. But he had courage, and tried his luck at everything. Eventually his time came to strike it rich: he came to Moon Mountain, at first only to harvest herbal medicine. But one day on the slopes he came across a tiger, and when most people would have run away as fast as they could, he followed it instead. And the tiger brought him to the hot springs.

Marigold laughed. "And then?"

"And then?" The vendor's wife flicked her cigarette away and kept on walking. "Then he made a fortune. I hear he has his own airplane. We're all just ants in the grass compared to him. No, I guess we aren't even that."

Marigold felt a stab of pain in her heart. She remembered walking behind the house with her husband and seeing those sharp spears of late sunlight advance through the valley and over her marigolds. She had felt the same pain then, and cried.

But this time, there were no tears. She had left her marigolds, discovered another world. That world was utterly alien to her, full of legends and transformations, and she couldn't accommodate. At this moment in her life, she had no idea how much she would need to change before she could become a part of it. The hot springs that were right under her nose might as well have been a million miles away.

As she thought on this, she felt a wave of anxiety.

She looked up into the cloudless night sky. What a beautifully full moon! The moonlight was so thick you could almost wear it for clothing. She suddenly recalled the man who was waiting for her under the moon – by the bend in the road before the forest. That man would give her a happiness that was visible and palpable. The world was as miserly as it was overwhelming, and beyond human grasp or comprehension. She had no reason to give up what fortune had offered her.

Marigold sighed to herself, then hugged her arms and sucked hard on her cigarette. The tobacco was poor quality, and the smoke had a dirty, confused flavor. Yet it didn't matter what kind of cigarettes you smoked under a moon like this one, only what you were thinking about. Looking back, the vendor's wife teased her, "Hey, what are you standing there for? What are you looking at? What's in the moon? Are there piles of money up there?"

"There's a hot spring in the moon," Marigold replied. "See for yourself."

The vendor's wife took a close look. What do you know – now that Marigold had said it, she really could see the rippling surface of a body of water up there. What could it be but a hot spring? But so high up! Women couldn't go there to tempt and tease, men couldn't go there to buy their pleasure. It was cold, blank, like a temple lantern, shining down on a world of sin unchanged for a thousand years.

A great bank of fog rolled over the two women. Beads of moisture scattered down like a fine rain.

When the fog receded, only one woman remained. It was the vendor's wife. Her skin and clothing wet with mist, she looked around in alarm but caught no sight of Marigold. She yelled out, "Hey—," but stopped herself. What are you doing? she thought. You don't even know her name. She seemed to remember Marigold saying something to her amid the fog, but her mind was somewhere else  and she hadn't heard clearly. She looked around once more, swore, then wiped the rain and mucus off her upper lip and tramped home.

When the fog first rolled in, Marigold had noticed a long, narrow wooden bridge spanning the river. She told the vendor's wife in an almost offhanded tone that she wasn't going to the hospital, although she didn't say why, and the vendor's wife – who didn't even hear her – didn't ask.

She crossed the bridge amid the fog, and was delivered onto another road. This road was dark and slippery, and to walk along it and watch the bright, extravagant colors on the other side of the river was a strange feeling.

After a while, she returned to the road she'd followed here. The stone bridge she had once crossed seemed to tower above her, a huge black shape silhouetted by the lights of the resort. It had just tasted human blood, and glowered menacingly at the world. Marigold felt grateful she would never have to cross it again.

She walked back up the long, winding road in the middle of the night. She came through the forest to the place where she and Miao Shanlin had separated. All she had to do was stop and softly call out, "Hey!" and the one-armed man appeared. He had been sleeping under a large tree. He had put grass and hay down on the ground, and sheltered himself on the far side of a boulder. In a place like this, one didn't need a boulder to hide oneself from view. This was the nest he had made for the night. Knowing Marigold would sleep there with him, he had dutifully laid his jacket out on top of the hay. The scent on his jacket wasn't very much like her husband's, Marigold thought to herself.

They slept until morning sunlight poured through the forest and fell on their faces. It was an intimate morning, though also a morning of separation. Everything went smoothly, just as Miao Shanlin had said: he got Marigold, and she got all the money he was carrying. Now he was penniless again, and had to take another road to find his livelihood, while she took the same road back to her village.

They gathered their respective bags. Just before they parted, Marigold took a packet of dried marigolds from her bag and gave it to Miao Shanlin as a gift. She felt that the flowers along with her body were a more even exchange for his money.

The sun rose, filling the earth with its light. Miao Shanlin turned east, and Marigold turned west. Miao Shanlin walked into the wet morning sun, contentment and happiness visible in his face. The night before his sky had shimmered with the stars of love, which had watered his desiccated life until it was full, ripe, and could no longer be seared by the fire of his heart.

Marigold went west. The sunlight pressed down heavily on her shoulders, and its heat bit into her like thorns, like she were carrying the love of a strange man. She unslung her pack from her shoulders and held it tightly in front of her, as the corners of her mouth crept up in a satisfied smile. She did not look back at Miao Shanlin; the man had been a gust of wind, which brought her an opportunity for happiness even as it passed through her life. It was as if she could see her husband's brilliant smile, and those wonderful early days had returned.

Marigold's feet carried her along a beeline back to her home, sometimes with such strong intent she broke into a run. With her hands grasping the pack at her chest, it looked from afar as if she had no arms.

*Translated by Canaan Morse*

徐皓峰

# Xu Haofeng

Xu was born in 1973 and graduated from the Beijing Film Academy in film directing. He won the Best Screenplay award at the 33rd Hong Kong Film Awards, the Best Action Choreography award at the 52nd Golden Horse Awards, and the Best Artistic Contribution award at the 41st Montreal World Film Festival.

师父

# The Master

### By Xu Haofeng

## 1

"The secret to fighting is… the head cannot hide. Hand is always faster than head."

Thus declared the young man with the battered face sitting in Jensen's Coffeehouse in the concessions of Tianjin, 1933.

Far behind him sat a Japanese woman, her neck pale as lotus root above a white floral kimono. His name was Geng Liangchen and he was clad in the plain jacket and trousers of a street peddler. Seated with him were two middle-aged men, their hands weighty on the table, knuckles callused and burnished from years of practice with punching bag and post.

The two wore formal robes of fine cloth. Tianjin's martial arts schools were sponsored by the rich and powerful, and a teacher's monthly salary could buy one hundred *jin* of beef. The pair's contempt for the younger man was clear.

"Don't believe me? Hit me! Come on!" Geng stood and motioned for one of the two to engage him. The older men glanced at each other before one obliged, standing to throw a mock punch, without speed or power.

Grinning, Geng grabbed the other man's fist and moved his head to the side as he guided it towards his own face. "See! Wrist is thin, neck is thick. So which moves faster, head or hand?"

"Hand," the other man said with exasperation.

Geng smiled like a father chivvying his child. "And again!"

Glaring at Geng, the man threw another slow punch. Geng did not evade it but punched back, his fist connecting with the ribs of the other man, whose own punch stopped short of Geng's face. "A head can't beat a hand," Geng said. "But a hand can."

Geng's sparring partner took two steps backwards and bowed, right fist cupped in left hand. "I am grateful for the lesson," he said, eyes brimming with hatred.

The seated man spoke, in a tone neither proud nor humble—martial arts centres always have these sorts of people: "An hour ago, in the school hall, he lost to you. According to the rules of the martial guild, the challenged play host to the challenger, victorious or otherwise. You insisted on this foreigners' coffeeshop, and we complied. What need to humiliate him again?"

Geng: "What are martial artists to talk about, if not martial arts? Am I wrong?"

"I'll fight you again!"

The anger of the older men could no longer be contained. Yet Geng returned to his seat and drained the dregs of his coffee. "I've only been training for a year, and my head keeps getting hit, what with not moving it. And with all the fights this month, my teeth are a bit loose. Perhaps you could wait ten days or so, to let them settle?"

"I'll pay for gold teeth!"

One threw a punch but immediately took an open palm under the ribs and fell stiffly back, unable to even gasp. His companion rushed to raise the stricken man's torso, placing knees below his vertebrae and arching his neck and jaw upwards. A puff of breath into his mouth and the victim cried out in an infant's wail.

He was conscious again, but his limbs were still useless and it was some time before he could stand. Two waiters watched from behind the counter – why are the waiters in Japanese coffee shops always old? The woman in the kimono on the other side of the room now stood, her face powdered deathly pale as a porcelain doll.

Geng stared, hand over mouth, at how his opponent had been resuscitated. "That's… incredible."

"It's nothing," the man said, enmity forgotten in his haste to aid his colleague. "Any martial artist can do it. Your master has not taught you?"

Geng shook his head. "My master…" Seeing the hatred return to the other man's eyes, Geng stopped and made his way to the door, hand still over his mouth.

A call from behind: "Do you want those gold teeth?"

The street was dreamlike through the frosted glass of the café door. Geng paused a moment then pushed out onto the street.

# 2

"How am I meant to change your sheets if you're lying there? Get up!"

"Come over here, I'll show you how to do it."

"Ha!" she scoffed.

He had been flirting with the landlord's middle daughter for a while now, lying on his bed and worrying his teeth. The landlord had three daughters, each arousingly plump and, like the descendants of fishing folk they were, not scared of a proper flirt. Even relishing one. Tianjin was a city of water, after all – salt flowed from its harbour up its nine rivers and into the veins of its people.

The eldest of the three girls had wed half a year since. Geng often told the middle daughter he had slept with her big sister.

The landlord's wife yelled from the yard, demanding her daughter hurry up and fetch the shopping. The fried cakes of Earhole Lane, their skin crisp and golden and their red bean filling as soft as fresh fruit, were the old woman's sole gastronomic pleasure. She declined an evening meal, fearing poor digestion would prevent sleep, but three in the afternoon was fried cake time.

The landlord's middle daughter: "Enough!"

She stepped forward to the bed and Geng leapt up to meet her. The girl instinctively folded her arms over her chest as she walked into Geng's embrace. Geng fled for the door as if scalded. That was as much liberty as he dared take.

"Off with you," she told him, bending to change the sheets.

Her buttocks rolled, her hips flared. Some older lads had told him girls got thinner when they married. He stared at her waist until he felt unwell, like when he drank too much water after running, and turned to leave, shouting: "I'll sleep with you too, the night before your wedding."

She did not hear. He left the boarding house.

She was not the one he liked. He had a book stall.

In 1922 the publication of *Marvellous Warriors of the Rivers and Lakes* in southern China marked the birth of the martial arts novel. By 1933 the "five northern masters" were in the ascendant and Li Shoumin's *Zu Warriors from the Magic Mountain* was at the peak of its popularity, both serialised in the newspapers and published by the chapter as each new instalment was written.

A chapter ranged in length from 20,000 to 60,000 characters and could be rented from Geng's stall for one cent a day, with a twenty-cent deposit. Geng also carried works by the other four masters: Bai Xiang, Zheng Zhengyin, etc. But it was Li Shoumin who brought in the money. A family of five in Shanghai, with two working adults, could stay warm and fed on 33 dollars a month. In Tianjin, you needed 14 dollars. Geng was single, so 7 dollars was sufficient.

He had a pitch on North Road, on the western side of Beihai Mansions, itself home to shops and, on the third floor, a teahouse. Tianjin's water was brackish and had to be boiled, though it was cheaper to buy boiled water from a stall than make it at home. Teahouses, with their ready supply of boiled water, were a second home for northerners. Regulars brushed their teeth and cleaned their feet there.

Teahouse customers rented books from Geng to read upstairs. Others stopped at the stall to read, Tianjin folk preferring to spend time on the street than at home. The tools of his trade were a pushcart on which to display the books, and five stools. Five were inadequate, but he provided no more. Any additional customers could lean against a wall.

Previously, Geng had been a porter, helping people move home or transport goods. His master had suggested the change of career, saying hard physical labour was no longer wise. The heavy lifting after martial arts training would drain all his energy. He would be as good as dead.

"That master of mine…" he sighed again on his way to Beihai Mansions. His master had paid for the seventy books he now lent out, for which Geng owed him a mountain of gratitude. And having now successfully challenged eight other schools, Geng had acquired the natural humility of the successful… he'd never thought life could be this glorious! Yet lately he had this strangest sense that his master… wanted him dead?

"What a thought! You're an ingrate! Dishonourable! Geng Liangchen, I'm ashamed of you!" He slapped himself across the face. Tianjin folk treat the streets as extensions of their homes and pay no mind to the stares of passers-by. He slapped himself again.

He had met his master a year ago. The 23$^{rd}$ day of the 3$^{rd}$ lunar month, the temple fair at Goddess of the Sea Temple. He was still a porter then.

The porters had "watchers", responsible for keeping an eye out for merchants attempting to move their own goods. If one was spotted, other nearby porters would be summoned to surround the merchant and insist on doing the work at extortionate rates. If the merchant had enough of his own men on hand, a mass brawl would ensue. But the porters were of poor backgrounds and despite their shady practices, had kind hearts. Old folk hurt in a fall would be carried to the doctor; ruffians harassing women sent packing.

The temple fair was popular with women, and every year this would lead to incidents. During dinner one of the watchers told him a gang of ruffians had spotted a woman of particular beauty and attempted to trail her and her husband home. If they had learned where the woman lived, the consequences would have been catastrophic. But her companion tackled all seven of them, his fists too fast to see, a foe falling with every blow.

There were many martial arts schools in Tianjin, and an expert displaying his skills in public was nothing new. But a woman that beautiful? Geng was intrigued. Tianjin's women followed Shanghai fashions, and beauties were common on the street. Was this one such a novelty?

The following morning he bought a pack of Three Castles and proceeded corner by corner, pressing a cigarette on every watcher he saw. Half a pack later, he had found the couple.

Three Castles were cheap and he grimaced with each draw. Their home was a single room, unshaded and opening onto the street. Knee-high brambles marked off a yard; sawdust carpeted the front of the house. A carpenter's bench and an unvarnished cabinet sat below a tarpaulin awning.

He saw the woman. She stepped over the threshold, discarded a handful of sunflower seed husks, and went back inside.

The husks glistened, snowflakes in the sun's blaze. The woman had a small face, a delicate figure, a neck as proud as a lotus stem.

He stepped over the bramble fence. "Is anyone at home?" he called. The woman came out and fixed him with her gaze.

These were not the bright eyes of a young girl, nor the coquettish eyes of a brothel whore. They were distant mountains, misty yet unyielding. He heard himself tell her he had come to challenge her husband to a fight.

With an attitude of great indifference, she performed the courtesies of great friendship. "Wash," she told him, fetching a basin of water. "My husband will return, but not for some time."

He washed. Four hours later her husband became his master.

He waited for an hour before her husband returned, carrying eighty crabs. Tianjin's many rivers mean crabs are cheap, a staple even for those too poor to buy flour.

The man washed as his wife went to boil the crabs. By the time the crabs were cooked, Geng had been floored forty-odd times, his nose was bleeding and his eyes swollen into walnuts. The man was panting somewhat, sweat running from his brow.

Street fights were the norm and any porter could handle himself. Geng was a quick and brutal fighter who, in the thrill of a mass brawl, would bring a particular target to his knees even if it meant a chase through the streets. "Like a pig that can't stop eating," his colleagues told him.

And there he was, being beaten like a pet monkey. He tried all the dirty tricks he disdained: he threw sand, he drew his pocketknife. For the first time in his life he wanted to kill someone.

The man told his wife to lay out the food. Patting Geng's shoulders, he apologised, explaining he had been to buy crabs by the riverside and needed to work up a sweat to expel the humidity, and had therefore fought a little longer than necessary. He went on to praise Geng for his well-proportioned frame and natural agility.

Geng hid his resentment. Like a child, he did what he was told; like a child, he tried not to cry as he did it. She handed him a cloth and he wiped his face; he passed him some crabs and he ate.

Geng ate twenty crabs, the man ten, the woman fifty.

Anyone who rarely gets meat will have a good appetite, and a working porter can eat two *jin* of rice in a single meal. But how could she eat fifty crabs? These were no mere sunflower seeds. Yet there was no fat on her – thanks to her being married, he knew.

"Given your frame, it would be a waste not to learn fighting. Why not study with me?" the man asked, once the crabs were finished. Still confused from his thrashing, he just kowtowed and accepted this new master.

His master's name was Chen Shi, his master's wife Zhou Guohui. Guohui? "National flower?" Surely too proud a name?

The west wall of Beihai Mansions, with Geng's book stall set out below. On the stools, two students and a former Qing civil servant. Next to his stall there was a stall selling *chatang*, a sweetened mush of sorghum flour, made with hot water from a large copper kettle with a dragon's mouth for a spout. The *chatang* girl watched his stall for him sometimes.

She was five years his junior, but he didn't let that prevent him taking advantage. Today he would have her watch his stall while he went home for a nap. He had been getting sleepy during the day, just like an old man, ever since his teeth were knocked loose.

She was plump in waist and thigh, pale as a Japanese doll, with ink-black eyes. She would smile when Geng walked over, revealing straight white teeth. He liked that about her, her teeth. Good teeth, bright red gums – good stock, that meant, a long line of healthy ancestors.

He was healthy too. Since starting training he often dreamed of his ribs, twelve pairs of them, white and strong, like elephant tusks. Health is like magnetism: a certain attraction exists between two healthy people. Or so he concluded from observations of his master and his wife.

Perhaps their mutual good health would see him and the *chatang* girl marry and have children. But he would not be able to tolerate her day after day, and he would die young. Just before passing away, he would whisper into her ear, "All that training wasn't wasted. Remove my ribs and sell them to the foreigners as elephant tusks."

His twelve pairs of ribs would be sold as elephant tusks for a fortune. The *chatang* girl could afford to smoke opium, gamble, keep lovers, and still have riches to spend. But she was a good woman and would live a frugal life until, an old widow, she passed away herself, a kind smile on her face and the money wasted. Over and over he imagined these scenes, particularly on seeing the *chatang* girl, never failing to be delighted.

She noticed him grinning as he stared at her. "What's wrong with you?" she yelled. Two bouquets of red lines appeared on her face as she shouted, the same red lines found on the ripest of apples and peaches.

He walked over and she retreated to her *chatang* stall. He sat behind his own stall. That had been no real meal; his fantasies were thin fare. But as he looked out over the bustling crowds he spurred himself on: plenty of schools to challenge yet, and you're the future of your art.

His master had estimated it would be three years before he could challenge other schools. But he was more talented than his master thought, and it took only one.

Tianjin had nineteen martial arts schools, each with ten to twenty pupils on average, which meant tuition fees were far from adequate to keep these schools running. But it was not pupils that mattered – it was the teachers. The nationalist government had encouraged martial arts from the very start of the Republic, to boost national pride. But apart from the arrival of the martial arts novel, the impact on the ordinary people was minimal – they were too busy working or enjoying themselves to study martial arts.

To retain the teachers, politicians and merchants made donations to these schools. But that meant more and more masters, and the emergence of an increasing number of previously unknown fighting styles. Geng's teacher was a practitioner of one of those lesser-known styles.

The night before Geng's first challenge, he had eaten crabs with his master, who had explained that public interest was not necessary for something to flourish: painting and porcelain-making were sustained by rich and powerful patrons. The same was true of martial arts. But martial arts could not be bid over and collected like a painting or a vase, and would die out when the political need disappeared.

Martial arts had been forbidden to ordinary people during the Qing dynasty, and their current popularity was an opportunity not be missed for less well-known schools. But Geng found himself asking what the point was, if they were bound to disappear?

"A lack of fame, our fathers' shame," his master said. "You won't understand now, but when I'm dead and you're the only one left, you'll know what that 'shame' means."

His master's expression – the apprehension and ambition of the long-term planner – convinced him.

Much of martial arts, like technology, was for show. Northern officials, despite knowing that the southern schools were as empty as their northern counterparts, organized trips south for northern masters. Billed as "Seven Tigers Going South" or "Nine Dragons Fly to Guangzhou", the northerners would spend two to four weeks teaching local students and generating publicity.

But what's the point of undeserved fame? The government had been promoting martial arts for twenty years, and martial arts attracted pupils regardless of their worth. Geng's master practiced Wing Chun, a school of few practitioners originating in Fujian, and had opted to come north alone.

There were more martial arts schools in Tianjin than any other city, and success in Tianjin meant national fame. Geng had guessed his teacher's plan: pose as a carpenter while learning about the various schools, then choose a local pupil to avoid north-versus-south sensitivities.

But what would he do next? There were nineteen schools in Tianjin; how many had to be beaten? What was the endgame once fame had been won? Presumably it was not just a case of getting famous and open-

Illustration by Wang Yan

ing a school – the most straightforward of plans were the riskiest.

A team of porters hauling a load went past, his friends of old amongst them but not acknowledging him. The cart he used for his stall belonged to the porters' guild. The porters' boss paid out daily, but there was an understanding that if you left after three years you had to buy your freedom from the guild. Geng had paid that himself, rather than mention it to his master. He hated to hand it over, those savings from years of hard toil. And he kept the guild's cart.

The cart was not worth anything and the boss had not come after it. But guild rules are guild rules: the porters ostracised him.

After five successful challenges he wanted to take them drinking. Not to flaunt his winnings, but to ease his sense of isolation. He would have spent every cent he had on them, but he knew they would not come.

He punched the cart as he watched his former brothers disappear. Nature offers no shield against predators, and the greatest protection for any wild animal is its pack. Now, because of this worthless cart, he was alone, with no one to run to or shelter with.


He kept the stall open past dark, relying on a lantern and the streetlamp thirty feet off. Neither gave off much light, and an hour later, weary eyes forced his remaining customers to quit. And that was a day's money earned.

A group of tearoom patrons came past on their way to a nearby restaurant, in search of a more substantial meal than the snacks and noodles the tearoom provided. One returned a book as he passed; another spoke to Geng: "I hear you challenged another school?"

He avoided that kind of talk, unwilling to be fodder for common gossip. He had done nothing to concern people of note, his reputation of no worth except to the street ruffians who now bowed as they passed his stall, true respect in their eyes. But there could be no friendship there – the martial guild and the street gangs were opposing forces, each keeping the other in check.

Perhaps his teeth were not that loose, and he was merely using it as an excuse to delay that ninth challenge. Although that thought gave his teeth a twinge. He'd eaten nothing but gruel for a week or more now. He cringed at the sight of a steamed bun.

A bowl of *chatang* would be good. Rock sugar sprinkled on the sorghum paste. Boiling water poured in and stirred. A sweet scent for five paces around. The *chatang* girl was watching him. She was always watching him, and he was always taking advantage. A nod of his head and she would rush over with a bowl, not bothering to charge him.

Just as he was about to give that nod, a rickshaw man stopped at her stall. The rickshaw men had once been part of the porters' guild, but with the Japanese – who had invented the rickshaw – building a factory in the city the number of rickshaws had increased and separate guilds had formed.

The rickshaw man, sturdy but baby-faced, ordered a bowl of *chatang*. Geng resented him on sight and turned to light his lantern – and then a chill at the base of his neck, the muscles of his back tensing inwards, an umbrella closing. A sense of a real threat, an animal-like intuition, something only acquired during his recent fights.

Look again. Careful.

The rickshaw man was eating his *chatang*, his eyes dark and predatory under a felt cap pulled low.

But squatting. Legs loose. Not a fighter's stance.

Ha.

Geng Liangchen, you're getting paranoid. That's what happens when you hide yourself away. Remember, you're the future of your art.

## 3

It was a time of "all masters and no pupils". Each school had a master – but no successors. Or so said Zheng Shan'ao, Tianjin's senior Bagua master, and the sole recipient of a visit from Chen when he arrived in Tianjin.

Building a reputation needs long-term planning. Earning fame in a single fight happens only in kung-fu novels – in reality, it takes three to five years, most of that in preparation and, if successful, following through.

Chen's sending Geng to challenge other schools was part of a plan. His eighth successful challenge was as much as Tianjin's martial guild could tolerate. One of the masters would have to take him on, for the sake of the city's reputation. That master would expel Geng, a rogue pupil, from the city, but Geng's victories would stand. The fruits of that success would fall to his master, Chen, who could now step forward and start his own school.

This was how minor martial arts schools grew. The challengers were sacrificial: a man destroyed, a school founded. And key to the plan was the master who would emerge to restore order. It was essential this man was an elder, respected by all schools. For this task, Chen chose Zheng Shan'ao.

There were two sides to Zheng: wile as a survivor of guild politics; sincerity as a true lover of the martial arts.

On the "Nine Dragons Fly to Guangzhou" trip two years earlier, Zheng was head dragon. Chen procured an introduction and offered to demonstrate the Wing Chun style for the honoured guest. Wing Chun has only three forms, each brief and lasting less than a minute performed at speed. Chen commenced with the first form, the "Little Idea". Zheng stopped watching halfway, dipping his head to sip tea. The audience was over.

Chen's patron was bitter at Zheng's scorn for the southern style, but Chen himself knew better, and returned home to wait. Three days later, Zheng came alone at night. "How," he asked as he stepped through the door, "did you learn Bagua moves?"

The Bagua the public sees is constant flowing movement. But in private, practitioners train with long sessions of motionlessness – and as in Wing Chun's "Little Idea" form, do so with feet splayed inwards and thighs pressing together.

The human body is a natural absorber of energy, and even the most powerful of punches will be cushioned by flesh and muscle, at best lacerating the skin. But with long practice in standing, the fist can acquire penetrative force, bypassing blood and bone to strike internal organs directly. The necessary stance is known in Bagua as "Horse Stance"; in Wing Chun it is "Goat Rustler's Stance".

Chen would hide nothing from a true master. Wing Chun's third "Thrusting Fingers" form, with its sneak attack on the opponent's eyes, was not for outsiders. "Keep the fingers indoors", the rule went. But Chen demonstrated it for Zhang, who paled: the principles were identical to Bagua's "Silken Brow Wipe".

The "Silken Brow Wipe" was Bagua's move of last resort, taught to Zheng by his own master. A mere two uses had assured his reputation for a lifetime.

Zheng sighed: "I used to wonder when I was training as a youngster... could it be that no other school had discovered these techniques? But it's only today, after thirty years, I've seen someone else use them.

Nature's secrets are there to be found, they say – and some of you Southerners did."

That night, Zheng's sincere love of the martial arts was in the ascendant, and he and Chen swore an oath of brotherhood.

A friendship based on gain will often end in betrayal; a friendship based on learning can be relied upon. Six months later, Chen arrived in Tianjin, not hiding his intent to earn fame with Zheng's help. Zheng did not welcome him with a restaurant banquet – the chance of being seen was too high. If Zheng was to later restore order by defeating Chen's pupil, their friendship must remain secret.

Zheng opted to welcome Chen at the Bei'anli Club – a French casino, not a place frequented by members of the martial guild. One of Zheng's pupils, an adjutant to a military governor, allowed Zheng use of his account at the club. Zheng would sometimes pass a night losing at the tables, but on this occasion he guided Chen, with great solemnity, to the casino's dance hall.

There was a can-can performance, the dancers mostly White Russians. The Russian revolution had sent many aristocrats fleeing to Tianjin, where they soon fell on hard times. After the can-can came a Georgian folk dance.

After the scantily-clad can-can performers, Chen was somewhat surprised to see a dancer in tall hat and long skirt take the stage. Her skirt reached the floor, hiding her feet, and she seemed to glide across the stage, her body motionless as she twirled.

The girl was eighteen or nineteen, the most beautiful of ages, and as poised as an empress. Despite doing no more than gliding about the stage, she won more applause than the can-can dancers. She was extraordinary.

But the dances had to titillate. After she'd made five or six circuits of the stage, a male dancer tore away her skirt. She danced on, thighs now shimmering silver. The secret to the dance, it transpired, was tiny rapid steps hitherto hidden under the skirt, and the muscles behind her knees flexing like swimming fish.

Chen's eyes displayed realisation. Zheng leaned in: "You see it?" Chen nodded. "Then we can go," Zheng said.

There was a garden outside, with benches for smoking and chatting. It was here the two came up with their plan to change the world.

"The schools are merely for show. They cannot get any pupils, and those pupils they do get are cheated. When I was learning, we were not permitted to talk to other pupils and took lessons individually. Now they do it in groups, defying a rule that has held for a thousand generations. What master would teach real learning in that way?"

"This martial arts craze is just a political game. And we're playing along."

"I'm not complaining about that. Bagua has a rule: in each generation, only three can be taught the true art. I do not know what it is they teach as Bagua today, but it's not Bagua. I can't stand to see it, but I promised to keep the secret when I started. There has not been one true fighter produced since the schools opened twenty years ago, because the schools are all fakes."

"Then when you said 'all masters and no pupils' – that was an insult."

"I am older now and see no points in insults. But there is something I wish to achieve. The politicians have no interest in genuinely aiding the martial arts. But what if we do it? Nature's secrets are there to be found, remember. That White Russian girl terrified me when I first saw her do that Georgian dance – the steps are the same as Bagua's 'Walking Circles' form. If we do not teach our people the true art, the foreigners will discover it sooner or later, and our children will never escape from under them.

"But Tianjin's masters will never reveal their secrets – if any of them did, the other schools would take revenge. An outsider has to be first to break the rules." The two were sitting side-by-side, but Zheng now turned to look at Chen and continued: "If you are willing to start a school and teach the true art, I will ensure the fame of Wing Chun."

Break his oath of secrecy? Chen was laid up in bed for a week at the mere thought.

On the eighth day Zheng Shan'ao invited him to Kiesling's, a well-known German restaurant. Chen accepted.

Chen needed to train a pupil who could defeat other schools. But before he found such a protégé, he found a woman: the waitress at Kiesling's that day, her neck as proud as a lotus stem.

Chen had sworn an oath, to teach the true art to no more than two pupils. Troubled by his decision to defy his master and break tradition, he failed to notice how much of Kiesling's free bread he was eating. On the seventh serving, the waitress intervened: "That's enough. I hate men who keep taking advantage."

Her eyes were distant mountains, misty yet unyielding.

A grand undertaking must change the world in some way. A man who would change the world is a man of passion. Zheng sighed as he watched how with one look, Chen was smitten.

Her uncle was boilerman for a church school; another more distant uncle was Kiesling's fruit supplier. And so she had grown up in the church school and now worked at Kiesling's. A girl from a poor family with no dowry to offer, her best hope was to catch the eye of a visiting German and be married off to Europe. It would not necessarily be, she knew, a young German.

Zheng Shan'ao visited her parents and negotiated her marriage to Chen.

In their home of Kaiping, Chen's family was known as the "99 buildings", for the number of properties they owned. But those had been lost during the military unrest. When Chen was younger and his family rich, he studied Wing Chun to improve his health, never imagining it would later be his only means of support. He had been a bodyguard for Nanchang merchants, served a brief stint with the Guangzhou police, escorted freighters across the South Seas...

Chen had some savings. But, at Zheng's suggestion, he moved his new wife into the slums.

Later, when his pupil started to challenge the martial arts schools, there was a flow of martial guild members calling to ask why he permitted such unruliness. "I cannot control him," was all he could say, and seeing he could barely provide for himself and his wife, they would accept this.

The poor are always busy. He learned some carpentry and soon, as is typical of the poor, became frantically busy and yet no better off. For Zheng, the marriage was a clever move: an idle wife will be assumed to mean a busy husband.

Chen was a man of the world and had enjoyed brief affairs. But when awakening in the night beside a lover, he often found himself repulsed by the stench of dissipation clinging to him. Yet on his wedding night, he sniffed himself: the fresh scent of rain-damp wood.

He could not tell her his plan. He simply slept with her night after night.

Nor did she think too much. He asked her once what she thought of him. "You're fine," she said.

He would happily have passed away in her arms. Let another generation concern themselves with Wing Chun's fame.

But then, as if it were fated, Geng Liangchen appeared.

Anything he taught to Geng, he first taught to Zheng. Gaining fame is easy, but keeping it is harder, and Zheng had not fought in earnest for fifteen years. It wouldn't be enough if the fight to come were merely a victory – it had to be both decisive and elegant.

Every few days, Chen left the house to "go and fix some windows." His felt cap pulled low, he would criss-cross the streets and alleys until sure no one from the martial guild was watching, and then head for Zheng's home, where he would knock at the back gate.

Zheng had the curiosity of a true lover of the martial arts and Chen found himself imparting more and more knowledge, far more than he taught Geng. Wing Chun has only three forms, but his master's generation had also adopted the short butterfly sword of the Qing navy. A fight on a cramped deck leaves nowhere to hide, and the sailors preferred blades designed to kill with a single stroke.

Chen's own generation had taken up the heaven-and-earth sword of the Jiangxi merchant escorts – two blades at either end of a handle, one slightly longer than the other, and crescent-shaped guards to protect the hands, the horns of the crescents facing outwards. If set upon by bandits, the escorts only fought if they had no choice, in which case they ensured the bandits retreated chastened and empty-handed. The heaven-and-earth sword was ideal for such a defence – clasp the central handle with both hands and parry easily to both left and right. If an enemy blade made it past that initial defence, the crescents could be used to block.

He had carried the weapon north, dismantled in its case. For the sake of Zheng Shan'ao, it now seemed. Each time he saw Zheng's joy in wielding the heaven-and-earth sword, he recalled how proud he had been to make that journey and wondered for a moment if perhaps Zheng was set to become the greatest beneficiary of this whole affair.

The tighter you grasp, the harder they grab. A Wing Chun motto, but true also in life.

The heaven-and-earth sword was kept at Zheng's. He never tired of practicing with it and Chen felt unable to reclaim it. As he left Zheng's residence one day, Chen became suddenly melancholy. The whole day spent on training... it would have been better spent with her.

Someone was selling a puppy on his route home, with a moving story: "I don't care about the money, I just want to find him a good home."

Chen approached and the seller beamed. "You've got a kind face. Just pay what you want." There was a round of haggling and Chen left, a pup in his arms.

The dog snuggled in the crook of his arm, a baked potato warming his heart. She would have company now, when he trained with Zheng.

A year later, as Geng Liangchen started to challenge other schools, the dog stood shin-high.

# 4

When martial artists negotiate, the manipulation of teacups can indicate their position. The overseers of the Zhongzhou and Xiayu schools paid a visit to Chen to inquire what his pupil was doing. The two schools were Tianjin's most powerful, the overseers second in rank only to the school heads.

"He is unruly," Chen admitted. "I have no control over him." The two visitors knocked their teacups against the edge of the tea-tray as they put them down. This meant trouble.

Events were again moving faster than planned. Tianjin's martial guild could not permit a ninth school to be defeated. Zheng Shan'ao would have to step forth soon.

Chen had never visited Geng's home, nor even allowed him to pay for a meal. He wanted no kindness from a sacrificial pawn. He saw his visitors out and, saying he was going to walk the dog, went out at the same time. He headed for Beihai Mansions and Geng's book stall.

In the end, he then turned instead towards the river, to buy crabs.

On the way home, water dripping from eighty crabs, he talked himself out of his guilt: "Big fish eat small fish, small fish eat shrimp. Fighting means the weak die and the strong survive, and we have to accept that fate. I do. Why should he not?"

He ate thirty crabs at dinner, she fifty.

Zheng was sixty-three and had all the vices of the young (late nights, smoking, gambling), yet greater strength. But he was old now, and the old are prone to panic and misjudge. Geng could end up crippled...

The cracking of crab legs jarred him. He had given her the legs from his share.

He craved her that night but restrained himself. She was full and drunk and slept with limbs outstretched. A clump of leaves floating in shallow water.

She was the reason Geng was studying with him. That first day, when he came back with eighty crabs, she sat on the threshold spitting sunflower husks, Geng watching her. Watching her the way he himself had, that day at Kiesling's.

Geng had started to train with him to see her. Chen could see what Geng was thinking, but believed this would change as he continued training, from the dignity of the art. And sure enough, he now averted his gaze from her, out of new-found respect for his master.

He ran his hand over her hip, as over the spine of a blade.

Zheng was a true lover of the martial arts, and a seasoned veteran of guild strife. A fight for his name would require him to be vicious. Geng could die...

He would wait till Geng was dead before taking her again.

Out of respect for how he looked at her, that first day.

As he made that vow, Chen was shaken by recollections of the oath of secrecy he'd taken when he was accepted by his master. As the sun rose, he clambered on top of her; she instinctively moaned below him.


Zheng's expenditure at the Bei'anli Club were covered by one of his former pupils, Lin Xiwen. Lin had joined the army after studying with Zheng, and now served as an aide to the military governor of Shandong, who was building a house in Tianjin and visited monthly to oversee the work.

That afternoon, as Chen entered the back gate to Zheng's home, Zheng was dressing to go out, in loose-fitting jacket and trousers of light grey. He told Chen these were made of the finest Ningbo silk, and had once been as white as snow.

Lin had brought a film camera on this trip, to film Zheng's "Shaolin Wall-Breaking" moves. All martial arts originate from Shaolin Temple, and a large mural there portrays forty pairs of monks at practice. To grasp all the techniques shown in that mural is to "break the wall".

Zheng knew nothing of the Shaolin style, but two months ago, having got carried away chatting with his pupils, had adopted similar Bagua poses to mimic it for a set of sketches. To his surprise this was treated as precious learning and published in the papers, where it was described as "revealing the secrets of the ages for the benefit of the people of today."

Lin spoke well of his master to the governor, who was fascinated and instructed Lin to have the moves filmed. If suitable, the governor said, these could be added to the army's physical training routine.

Zheng's white silk suit was tailor-made for his trip to Guangzhou, cut to flow elegantly as he performed. He loved it so much he wore it only twice. But white would not do for the filming – its brightness would unbalance the tone. He'd dyed the suit with incense ash, and it now looked like ordinary cotton.

"Such a shame!" he chuckled to Chen.

Seeing Zheng this excited, Chen was unable to plead mercy for Geng. There was still time, after all. He said he had come for training. "Another day," Zheng said, heading for the car at the main door.

A Ford sedan. The National Government had so many it was almost China's official car.

Some days later, Chen came back. The servant at the back gate said Zheng had not returned.

But the matter was now pressing. Chen had been summoned to the Zhongzhou school, and three other school heads were there too.

As Chen acknowledged his pupil was out of his control, the written notice would go directly to Geng. This meeting was to inform Chen that Zheng had been selected to administer the defeat.

Chen took his seat at the round table. No written notice was presented, but five cups of tea sat ready on a tray. Each of the four school heads reached out.

Chen knew what this meant. If the cup remaining to him was the one at the edge, there were no hard feelings.

The cup in the centre remained.

This meant war. There would be no official challenge. Geng would be dispatched, by any means necessary.

They watched him. To take the final cup signalled acceptance and the end of the meeting.

Sweat ran cold down Chen's back. "So many schools in Tianjin, and you four decide? What opinion does Master Zheng Shan'ao have?"

"Serving tea saves talking. Take it."

Chen reached for the cup. They were standing to leave before his fingers touched it.

# 5

Roof tiles lay like the plates of a warrior's armour. Zheng's home was a courtyard complex – one complete, two smaller, and one separate with its own entrance. There was no shortage of money in martial arts.

At the back gate, Chen did not knock but slipped over the wall.

Zheng had just dressed: a dark shirt and white Western-style suit.

He does like white, Chen thought.

Zheng sensed something was wrong and whirled, his eyes, to all appearances, threatening practiced violence. Then he smiled, display-ing three new gold teeth. Zheng had always been proud of his naturally strong teeth. He had competed with much younger men to strip the bark from sugar cane, and could peel a length of cane in a mere four pieces.

Chen did not ask what was happening, but Zheng spoke as he sat to pull on his leather shoes. "I'm leaving today, by boat. Hangzhou, then on to Guangzhou and Singapore. I need to pick someone up – we can talk in the car if you have something to say."

There was a for sale sign by the front gate, and an open-topped Ford sedan waiting. This was not a government car, but one Zheng had hired.

Zheng spoke as they drove into the concessions: "Tianjin no longer has a Zheng Shan'ao."

Legend has it that the dog-hawk lives in the borderlands of the south-west. When a young dog-hawk reaches maturity, it eats its parents. So it once was in the martial guild.

Most earned fame by fighting other schools. But if one's own master was renowned, he too could be challenged. This was known as "Thanking Teacher". No harm was seen in this: a defeated teacher would host a banquet to celebrate his success in passing on the school's arts.

But over the last twenty years, fighters had become celebrities and could not risk losing. "Thanking the teacher" was forbidden and young fighters could fight only their peers. To challenge an older fighter was treachery.

Lin Xiwen was a career man and did not practice regularly, so Zheng had never taken him seriously. But Lin had offered himself as sparring partner for the filming of the "Shaolin Wall-Breaking" moves, and was wearing a set of grey clothes cut to flow elegantly as he performed.

Zheng grinned at the sight of Lin, making it into the history books thanks to their association.

As one of the best martial artists of his day, any film of Zheng would be treasured by future generations. Zheng complimented his pupil: "Those clothes must be first rate to hang well standing or seated. But to look good as you move – that's the hard part. You must have taken some time over them."

Lin blushed.

Master and pupil, both elegantly dressed, took their places in front of the camera. There were forty-two moves in the set and all that was necessary was to perform them one by one. Yet Zheng, the veteran of over forty contests, had never been this nervous. Would today assure his legacy?

Suddenly he felt the end was near and his life held nothing but regret. There was much he should have done better. He should have become a father... Halfway through the set, Zheng performed "Old Man Casts Net"; Lin made contact with Zheng's elbow, in "Girl Opens Window".

The set of forty-two moves were slipping by as life does – action, reaction, over. Zheng felt worn out and even thought of stopping.

Lin's hand turned upwards at his elbow, no longer in "Girl Opens Window". They had only rehearsed for two days, and Lin did not know the moves well. But Zheng was confident he could manage the situation and ensure the governor would not notice the error...

When Zheng woke he was lying across two tables and missing three front teeth. The camera was gone, and two rifle-bearing soldiers stood nearby. Master Zou, of the Zhongzhou school, stood up from his tea and trotted over.

Zheng rose to sit on the edge of the table, his feet dangling half a yard from the floor.

This half yard might as well have been a mountainside. He could not get down.

Cut the earlier sections of the film, he knew, and it would seem like a real fight, not a demonstration. His legacy was to be the indignity of defeat.

"I fell for my own pupil's trick? He's in the army, not the guild. Why?"

"There's no point in asking why it's done once it's done. You know how our world works, my friend"

"But for what? The governor's favour?"

"Take this. He left it for you."

Zou pulled the ends of several banknotes from an envelope.

Zheng hung his head as Zou held out the envelope. "You won't take it?"

Zheng looked up, the empty gum sockets an infernal red. "Why wouldn't I take it? He's already taken my reputation!"

There were tables and chairs outside the door to the Bei'anli Club, and though it was not yet noon, a handful of White Russian men sat there. They were silent, arranged around two small tables, each with a cup of black tea.

"They never finish the tea," Zheng explained. "Or they would be asked to move on. But give them two silver dollars and they'll hand you a note with their home address, where you can have your way with their wife or daughter."

That was what the Russian aristocracy had come to. Zheng too was an aristocrat, the descendant of a top Qing general. His great-grandfather had died fighting the English navy on Zhoushan and earned the title of "brave *baturu*" – Manchu for "warrior".

Zheng was a man with an inheritance. But of that inheritance, only the house remained.

The person Zheng was to collect lived in the basement of the club. The croupiers and cooks were paid well enough to live off the premises – the basement was for waiters and dancers.

It was a White Russian girl, wearing the black headscarf of an old woman. Chen recognised her as the dancer of that Georgian folk dance, the muscles behind her knees flexing like swimming fish.

She had not fallen so far her father had to sip tea at the entrance. It must be costing Zheng to take her away.

She sat with Zheng in the car, carrying herself like any Chinese lady. Chen, feeling saddened, cracked a joke: "A wise plan! If we can't stop the foreigners stealing our secrets, we can steal their women!"

Zheng laughed heartily.

Chen spoke again: "But be careful, my friend. She's a lot younger than you. Mind she doesn't make off with your retirement fund." He looked at the girl as he spoke – these words were actually a warning for her. This might be the last time he would see Zheng, and the only thing he could do for him.

The girl could manage basic courtesies in Chinese, but as he looked into her eyes – and she held that look with eyes of lake-blue, as dazzling as church windows in bright sunlight – he had no idea if she understood.

Zheng looked at the girl with paternal affection and, after a moment, realised Chen's meaning. "She's always been poor, she's bound to look out for herself," he admitted. "But what's a man's money for, if not for women to cheat him out of?"

Chen paused a moment before smiling. Better to live for women and children, after all, than ideology and religion.

Zheng smiled in return; the smile faded to caution. "Forget fame. Return to Guangzhou, and take your pupil with you if you're feeling kind."

# 6

Geng sat at his book stall, looking out over the chaos of the street. He had done something he was ashamed of the night before.

His teeth were no longer loose, but he still needed a nap in the afternoon, like an old man. At noon the previous day, he'd asked the *chatang* girl to watch his stall while he had a nap – but instead, he'd gone to Xishui'ao.

His master was a southerner and thought crabs came only from the river. He did not know the best crabs were caught in the fields of Xishui'ao. When the sorghum was ripe for harvest the crabs crawled in, four or five for the plucking on each stalk of sorghum.

And these were meaty crabs, whether taken from river or field. He bought eighty.

His master was out when Geng reached Nannigu. Tianjin folk do not usually sleep on the earthen beds popular elsewhere. Instead they form platforms from boxes and boards, creating wooden beds large enough to sleep five or six. In the day that surface is used for eating and working, and has to be placed where the light is best, near the window.

The window was divided into two panes, the larger upper pane of mulberry paper, the lower five inches of glass – where might it have been scavenged from? An abandoned shop? A drinks cabinet a foreigner threw out, perhaps; drinks cabinets had glass doors...

Her face filled that pane of glass.

Geng panicked and ran, his eighty crabs thrown to children playing by the roadside.

He did not dare picture her face until he was back in his lodging. She had been in a deep childlike sleep; he could imagine her blooming as she slept. A smile lurked in the corner of her mouth, not the smile of a little girl but the tranquil smile of the Goddess of the Sea in her temple, bestowing beneficence on all aquatic life...

He lolled on his bed as if he had been dismembered. He did not notice when night fell.

When the streetlamps were lit the *chatang* girl collected up his seventy books and brought them to him. Most were slim volumes no thicker than a silver dollar, but he had to admire her strength.

Nor was it the first time she had packed up for him. He often took advantage like this, as if she was his long-suffering wife. She came in, tossing the bundle of books in her left hand to the floor. "Get up! You can pick those up yourself!"

He remained motionless. "If you could just do that for me...?"

She carried the bundle in her right hand over to the bed and, assuming he would duck, threw it at him.

His head did not hide. The books were not light and he rubbed his jaw, checking for loose teeth. The *chatang* girl panicked and examined his face for injuries, bringing herself within reach. Her pupils, always dark, seemed even blacker now, as if ground from the finest of inkstones and the oldest of ink.

He blocked her, heel of his palms on her shoulders. "I'm fine. Here, I'll show you something fun."

He went to the door and opened it wider, then pulled a contraption of rope and sticks from under a scrap of carpet. He slung it over the top of the door to hang down on either side.

He was now facing the edge of the door. From the top hung a rope, with four sticks attached at three points. At chest height, two sticks pointed towards him. To his abdomen, a single stick. Lower again, another stick angled towards his shins.

The four sticks represented an enemy's four attack points, for the practice of counter-attacks.

These sticks, fixed to a pillar, would be known as a "punching dummy". This collapsible and portable version was a "folding dummy". A punching dummy needed to be wrapped in wet cloth so force could be used; a folding dummy hung too loose for that, and served instead to practice varying angles of attack.

Practice long enough with a folding dummy and you will become as flexible as a snake.

This was a secret of the Wing Chun tradition. With only the open door to hang it on, Geng practiced only late at night, when the corridor was deserted, striking gently for silence. But now, for the *chatang* girl, he went faster, his knuckles rattling off the wood like walnuts.

This alerted the landlord's second daughter, who shouted as she descended the stairs: "What's all that noise, you idiot?"

"Get lost!" He removed the dummy and closed the door, to find himself gazing into the deep dark pupils of the *chatang* girl.

He had been trying to impress her. He did not know much about women, beyond having sort of held the landlord's second daughter. But he knew he wanted to hold the *chatang* girl much more firmly.

His moves were fast. One hand on her right flank, the other at the base of her neck. Wait, this was the start of a *qinna* hold. Was he fighting her? She bucked like a startled faun and pincered his neck between crossed forearms.

Her eyes were now hard black jade, darker than flesh had a right to be.

His hands fell. She flung open the door and fled, passing the landlord's second daughter on her way.

Where on earth, he thought as he massaged his throat, had a *chatang* girl learnt the Wing Chun "Closing Scissors" move? Just from watching him practice? His master said nature's secrets are there to be found. Could it be that all women…?

The landlord's second daughter seemed to be scolding him. He closed the door.

Sitting by the book stall, Geng decided he should not have done what he did. He looked over to the *chatang* stall. She was looking at him.

Had she already been looking at him? Or sensed his gaze approaching and turned a moment before to meet it?

Her eyes were no longer the hard jade of the previous night, but drying dots of ink on finest calligraphy paper.

And he thought of those other two dots of ink that he was sure had seen his true self through that scavenged glass.


# 7


Chen walked to Beihai Mansions, round the corner from Geng's stall.

With Zheng no longer offering protection, guild punishment for Geng was inevitable. As a former porter, Geng's only hope of escape was by hiding amongst the porters and their cargos.

Beihai Mansions had three floors. The ground floor was girded by an enclosed walkway, with shops every few steps. Three martial guild types stepped out of a doorway, blocking his path: "Master Chen, the Zhongzhou School invites you to tea."

Martial artists know the weak die and the strong survive. They therefore know to conserve their energy and rest when the opportunity arises, which means guild business proceeds at a gentle pace. He had thought Geng would not be dealt with for two days at least, and certainly not this soon.

The teahouse on the top floor had no private rooms. A group of guild members sat proudly in the main hall, the other customers paying them no mind. Master Zou bowed and invited Chen to sit.

Chen: "If both I and my pupil leave Tianjin and never return, could mercy be shown?"

Zou: "He goes, you stay. If we expel both master and pupil for beating eight schools… well, we'd look unreasonable. People would think Tianjin uncivilised. Stay, and we'll support your founding of a school. For a year, at least. We all gain face."

Chen: "And after a year?"

Zou: "If you still want to leave, we'll let you."

You could see Geng's book stall from the window. He was walking angrily towards the *chatang* stall.

Zou smiled: "We're the martial guild. Not politicians or gangsters. He'll leave alive. Hurt, but not crippled."

Chen bent to sip his tea, hiding a long sigh of relief.


Geng was not walking towards her. He was walking up to that baby-faced rickshaw man who'd kept coming back after that first time, watching her with hungry eyes from under his felt cap. He had not plucked up the courage to speak to her, but Geng had had enough.

Geng's kick sent Babyface's bowl of *chatang* flying.

Babyface's eyes darted to his rickshaw. The rickshaw men all kept a weapon hidden underneath their vehicles, in case of fights. Each profession had a favoured weapon: axe handles for the ruffians, a cart strut for the porters, and a rickshaw handle for the rickshaw men. All made of wood – no metal in street fights, or someone might get killed.

Geng: "Don't come back here again."

Babyface: "What gives you the right…?"

Geng: "I don't like the look of you." It was unfair, yet true. The rickshaw man had given him a bad feeling since their first encounter. "If you don't like it, ask around. I'm Geng Liangchen, defeater of eight martial arts schools."

Even he felt embarrassed for himself at that. Had that been necessary?

Babyface backed down and pulled his rickshaw away.

He had meant to repay the man for the *chatang*, but he'd left too quickly and was far away before Geng remembered to put his hand in his pocket. He wanted to shout after him, but... People got hassled on the streets every day. So what if he'd done it this once?

He looked back at the *chatang* girl. She stood glaring at him, lines of rage sprouting across her brow.

Geng: "I wasn't trying to lose you business, but that fellow... look, why don't you go and have a nap. I'll watch your stall."

Her: "I will!"

She left. Geng suddenly wanted to practice his moves, even for a minute.

A group of his old porter mates came past with their carts. He supressed the urge.

Five drinking *chatang*; six reading books. Just as Geng was thinking how good noontime business was, he saw Babyface coming from the west, a military officer in his rickshaw. They stopped by the stall and the officer ordered a bowl of *chatang*.

The officer was a sharp, hawkish man, and arrogant. "The book stall yours? Do you have Li Shoumin's new chapter? Fetch it if you do."

The new instalment was only eight thousand characters long. Word was that Li Shoumin was on holiday in Guangxi and sending his new chapters in by telegram, so each chapter cost as much as a thirty-five-piece set of mid-Qing mahogany furniture.

Geng walked over to his stall. The new chapter was in the hands of a customer on a stool. Geng squatted beside him: "There's an army gentleman would like to read that, probably just flick through it while he has his *chatang*. Could he borrow it a moment?" The customer narrowed his eyes dagger-thin and glared, and Geng continued: "And you read for free today, as many books as you like and no deposit."

The man held the book out, but when Geng reached for it, the man's fingers slipped from the book to seize Geng's wrist. The other five customers knocked Geng to the ground.

Only when he hit the ground did Geng gather his wits. He struggled and through a gap in his opponents saw the six customers from the *chatang* stall running over to kick him with their tough leather shoes. Soon Geng was immobile, bleeding from mouth and nose. Tricked, he thought. At least the *chatang* girl isn't here. I couldn't let her see me like this.

A crowd gathered, including both his porter mates and his ruffian admirers. A Ford sedan stopped nearby. The driver opened the rear door and Geng was dragged towards it. The street fell silent.

The roof of the car came to Geng's chest. He refused to bend and his assailants cursed as they beat at him, but Geng could not be forced into the car. Cheers were heard from the ruffians, and someone amongst the porters called out to him: "Do you need a hand, Geng?"

Geng laughed. "Not at all!" Recalling how the *chatang* girl had escaped his grasp the previous night, he jerked his body and shot his left arm outwards.

Just one hand would do. Penetrating blows, rapid changes of angle, close quarters fighting: this was the Wing Chun speciality. Chop necks, poke eyes, three down in seconds.

The officer and Babyface approaching, unhurried. Two more down, the remainder pressing closer.

Babyface flung aside the attacker to Geng's front. The officer stepped forward, slid two daggers into Geng's belly, like keys sliding into locks..

Geng folded over. Someone shoved, and he collapsed onto the back seat of the car.

# 8

The third-floor tearoom, still tranquil.

The foreign press complained local restaurants and tearooms were unbearably raucous and uncivilized. But such attempts to alienate the two populations were baseless. A cheap restaurant in any country will be as lively as a market fair, because in essence that is what it is. China's more refined establishments took pride in tranquillity, with both restaurants and tearooms as quiet as the night.

Looking down from the window, Chen did not see the daggers.

The sedan left, and the porters and ruffians drifted off with the crowd. Nobody minded the two stalls, nor did anyone touch them. Tianjin was, after all, a civilized place.

Zou, hollow, a little saddened: "Martial arts are for the schools, not the streets. There's no fighting back once you're pinned to the ground, regardless of how good you are."

Chen: "He's a Tianjin lad. Tianjin folk get homesick."

Zou: "Do not blame me. The army is punishing him, not the guild."

That army officer was Lin Wenxi, making a statement by handling a task that was rightfully the guild's responsibility, then striking the final blow both in person and in public. The Shandong military governor was now the patron of Tianjin's martial guild.

Zou: "First it was Zhili, now it's Shandong. Our generation are no more than ornaments. Too fragile for practical use, simply status symbols for our owners."

Tianjin was a port city, known for gun-running and drug-smuggling. The governor's intervention meant he wanted a share of these profits. The cost of funding the martial arts schools would be a drop in that ocean, and boost both his career and public standing. It would be foolish not to do so.

Zou: "The army was popular back in the first days of the Republic. Nobody had any faith in the gentry or the bureaucrats, but thought the army might improve things. These twenty years I've watched as the army became corrupt, and we failed to even notice as we became its playthings.

"The army only knows how to take money and territory. It does not govern, it campaigns. It tricks the public with 'national pride' campaigns. But when they campaigned to revive worship of Confucius or restore ancient rituals only the gentry approved; the students protested. The most reliable option is to promote the martial arts, that suits everyone."

During Qing times, martial artists were manual labourers, employed to guard convoys and courtyards. There had been no schools before the Republic. "My master's generation could not comprehend how rich we have become," said Zou, lifting his teacup. "And once you're rich, you can't go back."

Chen drank too. Only as the tea entered his mouth did he realise it had long gone cold. But they both drank.


The car drove west out of Tianjin. Lin had removed his cap and was driving. On the back seat, Geng was squeezed between Babyface and another soldier, also out of uniform.

The handles of the daggers piercing Geng's belly were six inches long, the blades a mere four. Such weapons would not reach any vital organs and were for incapacitating, not killing. The daggers could not be removed without Geng's intestines slithering out behind them, but handkerchiefs pressed to the wounds had stopped the bleeding.

Geng sat obediently and said nothing, beyond requesting not to be jolted about so much. "The road's bad," Lin told him. West of Tianjin was Langfang, where lines ran north and south of a railway station.

The car stopped seven miles from Tianjin, before reaching Langfang. Geng was lifted from the car. Less than one quarter of a mile away stood a brick-built church, a carving of two lions just visible on the wall, the crest of some country of other. He did not know which.

Lin: "There's a clinic at the church, go and find the doctor. Walk slowly, or the daggers will slice your guts to ribbons. Consider the walk my punishment, for wounding five of my men."

Geng: "How kind."

Lin: "When that's done take the train from Langfang. Go north, go south, but do not come back. That is the guild's punishment."

Geng: "I won't leave."

Lin: "I've killed two hundred bandits and rioters in Shandong alone."

Geng: "I've lived in Tianjin for twenty-six years. What kind of man would I be to leave my family and friends after one fright? How could I hold my head up anywhere else?"

Lin pointed at Tianjin: "That's the worst thing about Tianjin folk – they're all talk. Fine, show me what kind of a man you are. Run fifty paces that way."

Babyface snorted with laughter. Geng looked towards Tianjin: a leaden cloud of smoke, seemingly with nothing under it.

Geng was born in Tianjin, the oldest son of a poor family, kicked out at fifteen by his father to fend for himself. He had never gone home. He later heard his parents had taken his several siblings to the countryside for an easier life. He was the only member of the family left in the city.

Lin got bored of waiting and sat in the car. His henchmen released Geng and hurried to join him.

With a roll of dust, the car turned for Tianjin, Babyface driving, the other soldier beside him, Lin alone in the rear seat. The stench of blood was repulsive and, not being a smoker himself, he ordered the soldier in the passenger seat to light up and dispel the odour.

How dull life was, dragging everyone down to such actions. Lin was also twenty-six and had yet to meet anyone of any honour. The governor had none, his master had none. One with strength, one with guile, but neither with honour.

He settled his head back, hoping to sleep, when Babyface called out: "Boss, look!"

In the rear mirror, a tiny figure was in hard pursuit.

Lin twisted to see Geng collapse in the dust.

Babyface: "Should we stop, boss?"

Lin: "Running like that will have killed him." Geng lay still and shrank to become a speck of dust on the window. Lin turned and muttered at Geng's stupidity. Although… perhaps Geng was a man of honour?

Lin's assistant watched him fall asleep.


The streetlamps were on, but the *chatang* girl had not yet packed up her stall.

Instead of napping, she had made Geng a meal. Upon returning to Beihai Mansions, she heard of his abduction. A thousand scenarios presented themselves, but she told herself he would be back once the problem was resolved.

He had collapsed several times, but seven miles is no distance. Geng reached Tianjin, a felt rag wrapped around his waist concealing the daggers. The felt had been pulled from a passing lorry, where it was covering a basket of the hundreds of tonnes of vegetables Tianjin imported every day.

His plan for returning to Tianjin was to find the *chatang* girl, order a bowl of *chatang*, and on finishing it say: "That practice dummy is a secret of the Wing Chun school. Destroy it for me," And then, as his words hung in the air, to fall dead at her feet.

That was the best ending he could imagine for a Tianjin native: to be born in Tianjin and to die in Tianjin. But on seeing her, he realised how unsuitable an ending it was for him.

He was clutching a wall at a corner two hundred feet distant, watching her. He knew he was pale and hunched – he didn't want to die in front of her looking like that. And who said a man had to die in front of a woman?

He would not scare her like that.

Geng took one last greedy glance before turning to leave. He would memorise her in this life, so as to recognise her in the next.

He wanted to walk as far as possible and reached the fried cake-sellers of Earhole Lane. Having made it that far, he started to imagine he might survive. Geng felt his mouth – those loose teeth did seem better.

A team of eight or nine porters came his way, pushing a long cart stacked with three storeys of boxes: waste stock from the Zhengxingde Tea Shop, to be hauled back to the factory overnight.

Zhengxingde had four grades for tea: exceptional, fresh, strong and stale, with stale being unfit for consumption and rejected as waste. "That's what I am now," he smiled to himself. "Waste stock." He ran after the cart and squeezed in among the porters.

One recognised him: "Geng, you're not a porter any more!"

Geng: "I'm leaving Tianjin tonight. Let me join you for a while."

Three hundred feet later he slipped from the side of the cart and floated like a scrap of paper to the ground.

# 9

Northerners believe the death of a young bachelor is highly inauspicious, and no funeral procession should be held.

Geng was buried at night. The burial ground was in Xishui'ao; the sorghum fields nearby known for their crabs. Most porters never marry or have children, and this is where they too are buried. The porters had, in the end, accepted him.

Zou informed Chen that Lin had obtained the funds for Chen to open a school, and suggested he leave the slums and find a respectable place to live. "I'm used to it here," Chen said. "I think I'll stay."

Zou attempted to persuade him: "You've achieved your aim of making a name here in the north. Make a show of it! In your position I'd feel the same. But what's life if not putting on a show? And you have a wife, do it for her."

Perhaps in recompense for Geng's death, Lin had arranged a prime location for Chen's school, on bustling Dongmenli Street, with a large hall opening onto the road. The site had first been an apothecary, then split into two residences, and had twenty-two rooms. The apothecary had needed space to store and manufacture medicine, meaning there was a big yard perfect for martial arts practice.

Zou himself took charge of the opening of the school, managing each detail personally. It took him three weeks and he seemed to take great enjoyment in it, his colour improving daily.

He wrote by hand the programme for the opening ceremony, in a script both attractive and neat. Alongside the traditional rituals, there was to be a film-screening: the latest instalment of *The Burning of Red Lotus Temple*, starring Butterfly Wu, empress of the silver screen. Eleven school heads would be in attendance and all were keen to see it.

The day before his school opened, Chen visited a bank in the English concession, to retrieve the contents of a safety deposit drawer. He then went to a pawnshop, where he redeemed a leather suitcase containing two woollen suits and two pairs of leather shoes – he could not have kept such fine clothes while living in the slum, and the pawnshop aired clothes, guarded against pests and charged reasonable interest. A fine place to store clothes, as long as you could afford to redeem them.

Finally, he went to Xishui'ao to buy eighty crabs. He had at last learned the best place to buy crabs, having heard the porters talking when Geng was buried.

Back in Nannigu, where they still lived, he ate thirty and she ate fifty. Once the table was cleared he sat down to talk to her, only then realising how rarely he did so. She had been there for a year, like one of his limbs.

He placed the suitcase on the table and from below the suit and shoes removed a roll of banknotes and a box of pearls. There were over fifty pearls, unholed, acquired during his time as a guard on a South

Seas freighter in his twenties. On top of these he placed a train ticket to Qingdao, with a connection onwards to Guangzhou.

Him: "This is all my savings. Wait for me at the station tomorrow. If I don't come, take the train. You can go anywhere from Qingdao, it doesn't have to be Guangzhou. Wherever you want."

She was somewhat moved by the pearls and almost shed a tear. He had hoped for a fun evening in return, but they were both so full of crab that on retiring, they soon drifted off to sleep, each lying on their side.

Before leaving the following morning, Chen found he had more to say:

"The foreigners humiliated the Qing, and we Chinese lost our pride. People in the Republican government knew how important restoring that pride was, but promoting martial arts was the wrong choice.

"In a technological era, national pride should come from technology. But we don't make the best guns and artillery, or the best trains and boats, so we tried martial arts instead. But you can train for a lifetime and lose it all to one bullet. Martial arts don't mean national pride, but national shame.

"Opening a martial arts school would make me a conman. That's what I'm going to tell them today. They need to wake up!"

She was somewhat moved and almost shed a tear, much like with the pearls. She was not used to hearing him speak, and didn't have much to say in response.

Chen left.

He did not plan to say those things at the ceremony. They already knew.

Put on a show and everyone is happy. As the programme unfolded, Chen found himself pleased at his success, at having achieved his goals in coming north.

The ceremonies were due to start at one and end with an evening banquet at nine, on Palace Street. As that would require evening dress, events at the school would end at six, allowing time to return home and change. The final event at the school was to be the film, at half past four in the main hall.

The screen was hung in front of the shrine to the founders of the school and four rows of chairs set out. As a military man, Lin had pride of place in the centre, with the school heads then taking their seats in order of status. Boards were placed over the doors and windows of the main hall, rendering it pitch dark.

There was to be a short before the main feature. And… it was Lin Xiwen fighting Zheng Shan'ao. One minute and forty seconds, of which only twenty seconds were action. The remaining time was filled with title cards, in Lin's words, at the start giving the time, place and names of witnesses, at the end analysing why he had won. The cards were printed in the free and changeable running script style of Wang Xizhi.

Lin's sneak attack had been edited out. All that was left was Zheng taking a blow below the ribs but immediately counterattacking, his fingertips reaching Lin's eyes before stopping, with no way to tell if this was due to editing or a counter-move from Lin the lens had missed. Lin seized the chance to land a heavy blow to Zheng's jaw, followed rapidly by five or six more to the face.

The first blow left Zheng stunned, and only decades of training kept him on his feet. Bleeding from nose and mouth, he struck a fine pose and with dazzling speed dashed backwards ten feet. But it was one flash of brilliance before Lin closed the gap, swinging left and right like the foreign boxers. On the tenth blow, Lin could stand no longer and thumped to the ground like a side of pork.

The cause of Zheng's loss was the aborted attack on Lin's eyes. Chen recognised the "Silken Brow Wipe" and knew Zheng had balked at blinding his pupil.

The lights came up for the changing of the reels. The school heads twiddled their thumbs or gazed at the roof, but avoided each other's eyes. They all understood Lin's meaning.

Previously the army had funded the martial guild whilst allowing it to remain autonomous, with no military involvement. Lin meant to change that arrangement. Defeating Zheng gave him status within the martial guild as well as the military, and he would now take charge. The schools would serve him and the guild would be independent in name only.

The school heads had, over the last twenty years, seen the army hollow out the government, the parliament, the commercial guilds, the railways, the banks... How could the humble martial guild stand against such powerful forces? Better to accept fate and sit obediently, waiting for the Butterfly Wu film to start.

Chen, as host for the day, sat to Lin's right side. He stood, tore down the screen, and grabbed a blade concealed in the shrine behind.

The heaven-and-earth sword. Chen: "Where there is a school, there are challengers! Who accepts my challenge? This is my school. I suppose I have to accept my own challenge." He laughed.

This was ominous. But there's always one who thinks a bit too much of himself: a school head rose. "What do you think you're playing at...?" He was yanked back to his seat by those alongside.

Chen: "My pupil defeated eight schools. I want to defeat the ninth. Master Zou, do you accept the challenge?" Zou, sitting to Lin's left, smiled but did not answer.

Chen: "Who accepts?" No one spoke.

Chen walked to stand in front of Lin. "The vanquisher of Master Zheng Shan'ao. Will you accept my challenge?"

Lin forced a smile. He was not so arrogant to think he had trained diligently enough to stand and fight this man. But there he was, alone, challenging the entire martial guild... and yet he seemed unhinged, rather than admirable.

Lin: "Do not forget what your betters have done for you. Have you thought about what you are doing?"

This man, a decade and a half Chen's junior, with his fine eyebrows and strong brow, seemed to be of some superior race, representing some new pinnacle of history. But the treachery of a new generation is often how history progresses, and if no one can see how history ends, no one has the right to judge. Who is to say what will prove right or wrong?

When ideals are lost, violence can provide some comfort. Grand gestures are borne of inferiority, and Chen had long been remorseful of treating Geng as a pawn to be sacrificed in his quest for fame. No less than the others seated there, he had wished for Geng's early destruction.

But like his plans of finding fame in the north, his plans of revenge were, in the end, ridiculous. A fight to the death, trapped and outnumbered... a fine fantasy to drift off to sleep to, but was he to maim and kill all these people?

Zou stood and came to him, reaching tentatively for the handle of the sword. "Chen, my friend, put it down. We know the pain of losing a pupil. We can all pretend this was a bad joke."

Sweat broke out on his back, the post-fight weakness coming over him. Zou offered comfort: "Adjutant Lin won't take offence." Lin nodded in the darkness.

Zou took Chen's sword and guided him back to his seat.

Zou was unsure where to place the sword, with its blades at either end. Neither leaning it on the wall nor placing it on a table seemed appropriate. Seeing this, Chen spoke: "You need to remove the blades. Here, I'll do it." He reached out and, after a moment of hesitation, Zou handed it to him.

Those adjacent tensed as Chen dismantled the weapon, but soon relaxed. Lin looked on with interest as the blades approached his neck more than once.

The heaven-and-earth sword was known as the finest of defensive weapons, yet he had not been able to defend even his own honour... a tear fell to the blade, like a drop of the tung oil used to protect it.

A push of the thumb and the teardrop spread like a drop of that oil, permeating the blade to flow within it forever.

The others, seeing Chen's tear, looked away.

The sword became two short swords, two crescent guards and a chest-high staff. At a signal from Lin, Zou started the film.

The room fell dark. A title card appeared: "*The Burning of Red Lotus Temple*" based on the millennia-old script of the Northern Wei tablets, but with such intrusion of modern calligraphy it seemed contrived, half-painted and half-written.

A sudden clatter of chairs toppled and tables overturned.

The lights came on. Five or six men, Zou chief among them, held Chen pressed to the floor.

Chen was pulled to his feet, still under close restraint, each arm and leg held fast. Zou stepped apart and explained to Lin: "The man is disturbed and we worried he might cause more trouble. We could not relax with him at your side."

Lin smiled. He had long since tired of others currying his favour. He could not help but remember Geng Liangchen as he looked at them all. Ah, the guild would be much more interesting if Geng was alive.

Lin walked over to Chen, hoping to explain that Geng had died not at his hand, but due to his own stubbornness. But seeing Chen's reddened eyes, he kept silent. He really did appear insane. How should this delicate situation be handled? Should he be jailed, or returned to his wife?

As he pondered the question, Chen's left arm broke free and wheeled outwards before being seized and returned to the scrum.

And with that, Lin could not decide if he understood everything or understood nothing. One hand clasped to his neck, he walked fifteen paces and collapsed. A shame: if blood flowed more slowly, there might have been time for more answers.

His jugular had been sliced open.

Chen's free arm had wielded one of the blades from the heaven-and-earth sword.

Had he grabbed it while pinned to the ground, or had someone pressed it into his hand? He was not sure, and regardless, it was gone now, taken by someone skilled in disarming techniques. A brief touch and his hand was empty. Which school could that be?

The scrum loosened a little. The Wing Chun position utilising the strength of the spine is "Soaring Arms" and involves both left and right fists shooting outwards, felling all who are touched. His captors toppled like a collapsing wall, and Chen darted for the door.

# 10

Chen's wife had been sitting on Dongmenli Street watching the school for some time. She had not, as instructed, gone to the train station, as she was sure Chen could not die while she was within six hundred feet.

She had been keeping a secret from Chen: she had a child. Fathered by an American geography teacher at the church school, when she was fifteen. Had she liked him, or been forced into it? She was so young at the time it was hard to say now.

The American was a second-generation immigrant himself, of Hungarian and White Russian descent. The child had been taken off by the trafficker as soon as it was born, and all she saw was the green-black meconium, a clump of willow leaves drying on the floor.

She did not think of her baby till she was seventeen, and then couldn't stop thinking about it, to the point of obsession. Her uncle sent her to the temple to study Buddhist scriptures, where an elderly monk told her that as long as she kept her baby in mind, her baby would return. A mother's love transcends the cycle of death and reincarnation, and not even the Buddha himself can prevent that reunion.

And as Buddhist scripture taught, the strength of those thoughts can bring great virtue if turned to prayer.

She did not turn that strength to prayer. She used it to think of her child. And now, she used it to think of her husband.

He had appeared one day and changed her life. Women have to be with someone, so she accepted her fate. The clothes he bought her were worse than those Kiesling's had provided; he rarely spoke, just climbed on top of her every night. Had she liked him, or been forced into it? She couldn't be bothered to work it out.

She lived with him, but she had plenty of her own interests to occupy herself when he was out.

He came home with a dog one day, and since then she had used the dog to test the power of her thought. Dogs could be as smart as four-year-old children, they said, and can sense wandering spirits.

If she was within six hundred feet and concentrated on the dog, it always looked at her. She was not sure though. Perhaps the dog noticed her looking or some gesture she was unaware of.

But here on Dongmenli, she had to be sure of herself. If she was here, he was safe.

She was sitting in a bakery, which had the usual few seats for those who wanted to consume their purchases. Customers usually sat for only a few minutes before making room for others. But she had sat for four hours, with suitcases and dog at her feet. Her three pastry purchases did not offset the staff's irritation.

Perhaps what he said that morning had changed things. She knew it was all nonsense, but she was now sure: she had not been forced into this. She loved him.

With its doors and windows boarded up, Chen's school looked just like a closed apothecary's. Suddenly, the boards over the door blew outwards, tumbling to the ground like chopsticks. Chen sprinted out, others in pursuit, headed in the direction of the Goddess of the Sea Temple.

She ran after them.

Two streets later she had lost sight of both Chen and his pursuers, and her ankles were as hot and fragile as just-fried dough-sticks. She looked at the dog and thought of Chen. Barking, the dog ran into the crowds, leaving her far behind.

Chen had spent two nights learning the roads around Dongmenli. He headed away from the train station, then weaved through streets and alleys in a large clockwise circle until, just as the train was ready for boarding, he arrived there.

A month of planning, mostly to good use. He lacked only the pleasure he had expected from revenge.

She was not on the platform.

What had Zheng said? "What's a man's money for, if not for women to cheat him out of?" He smiled and then saw their dog bounding towards him, trailing puffs of dust. He bent to sweep it up in his arms; it was stove-hot.

She must have exchanged her ticket for an earlier one and abandoned the dog here.

The guard was urging passengers to board. He tucked the dog under his clothes and pushed on board.

When he sat down the dog started to bark and without thinking he removed it from under his clothes. A foreigner sitting across from him complained loudly that pets were not permitted on board.

Chen responded with a murderous glare. The foreigner fell silent and left in search of a guard.

He stroked the dog; the train pulled away. Leaving Tianjin forever.

*Translated by Roddy Flagg*

陈楸帆

# Chen Qiufan

Chen Qiufan (also known as Stanley Chan) was born in Shantou, Guangdong province. Chen is a science fiction writer, columnist, and online advertising strategist. Having previously worked at corporations including Google and Baidu, he is now vice president of Noitom Ltd, a company that focuses on motion capture and virtual reality. He has won numerous awards for his work, including nine Chinese Nebula awards, three Galaxy awards, and the SF&F Translation Award. Many of his short stories have been translated by Ken Liu, including "The Endless Farewell" and "A Future History of Illness", which have previously appeared in *Pathlight*. Ken Liu's translation of his novel *The Waste Tide* is forthcoming.

巴鳞

# Balin

By Chen Qiufan

*I judge of your sight by my sight, of your ear by my ear, of your reason by my reason, of your resentment by my resentment, of your love by my love. I neither have, nor can have, any other way of judging about them.*

—Adam Smith, *The Theory of Moral Sentiments*

Balin's dark skin, an adaptation for the tropics, appears as aphotic as the abyss of deep space, all reflected light absorbed by the thick layer of gel smeared over his body and the nanometer-thin translucent membrane wrap. Suspended between bubbles in the gel, microsensors twinkle with a pale blue glow like dying stars, like the miniature images of me in his eyes.

"Don't be afraid," I whisper. "Relax. Soon it'll be better."

As though he understands me, his face softens and wrinkles pile up at the corners of his eyes. Even the scar over his brow is no longer so apparent.

He's old. Though I've never figured out how to tell the age of his kind.

My assistant helps Balin onto the omnidirectional treadmill, securing a harness around his waist. No matter in which direction he runs and how fast, the treadmill will adjust to keep him centered and stable.

The assistant hands the helmet to me, and I put it over Balin's head myself. His eyes, bulging with astonishment like two lightbulbs, disappear into the darkness.

"Everything will be fine," I say, my voice so low that no one can hear me, as though I'm comforting myself.

The red light on the helmet flashes, faster and faster. A few seconds later, it turns green.

As though struck by a spell, Balin's body stiffens. He reminds me of a lamb who has heard the grinding of the butcher's knife against the whetstone.

#

A summer night the year I turned thirteen: The air was hot and sticky; the scent of rust and mold, prelude to a typhoon, filled my nostrils.

I lay on the floor of the main hall of my ancestral compound. I flattened my body against the cool, green mosaic stone tiles like a gecko until the floor under my body had been warmed by my skin; then I rolled to the side, seeking a fresh set of tiles to keep me cool.

From behind came the familiar sound of scuffling leather soles:

crisp, quick-paced, echoing loudly in the empty hall. I knew who it was, but I didn't bother to move, greeting the owner of those footsteps with the sight of my raised ass.

"Why aren't you in the new house? There's air conditioning."

My father's tone was uncharacteristically gentle. The new house he referred to was a three-story addition just erected at the back of the ancestral compound, filled with imported furniture and appliances and decorated in the latest fashion. He had even added a spacious study just for me.

"I hate the new house."

"Foolish child!" He raised his voice, but then quickly lowered it to a barely audible mutter.

I knew he was apologizing to our ancestors. I gazed up at the shrine behind the joss sticks and the black-and-white portraits on the wall to see if any of them would react to my father's entreaties.

They did not.

My father heaved a long sigh. "Ah Peng, I haven't forgotten your birthday. I had an accident on the way back from up north with the cargo, which is why I'm two days late."

I shifted, wriggling like a pond loach until I found another cool spot on the tiled floor.

The cigarette stench on my father's breath permeated the air as he whispered at my ear, "I've had your present ready for a long while. You'll like it; it's not something you can buy in a shop."

He clapped twice, and I heard a different set of footsteps approach, the sound of flesh flapping against stone, close together, moist, like some amphibious creature that had just crawled out of the sea.

I sat up and gazed in the direction of the sound. Behind my father, a lively black silhouette, limned by the creamy yellow light of the hallway light, stood over the algae-green mosaic tiles. A disproportionately large bulbous head swayed over a thin and slight figure, like the sheep's head atop the slender stick that served as a sign outside the butcher's shop in town.

The shadow took two steps forward, and I realized that the backlighting wasn't the only reason the figure was so dark. The person – if one could call the creature a person – seemed to be covered from head to toe in a layer of black paint that absorbed all light. It was as though a seam had been torn in the world, and the person-shaped crack devoured all light – except for two tiny glowing points: his slightly protruding eyes.

It was indeed a boy, a naked boy who wore a loincloth woven from bark and palm fronds. His head wasn't quite as large as it had seemed in shadow; rather, the illusion had been caused by his hair, worn in two strange buns that resembled the horns of a ram. Agitated, he concentrated on the gaps between the tiles at his feet, his toes wiggling and squirming, sounding like insect feet scrabbling along the floor.

"He's a *paoxiao*," my father said, giving me the name of a creature from ancient myths who was said to possess the body of a goat, the head of a man – though with eyes located below the cheeks, the teeth of a tiger, and the nails of a human, and who cried like a baby and devoured humans without mercy. "We captured him on one of the small islands in the South China Sea. I imagine that he's never set foot on a civilized floor in his life."

I stared at him, stupefied. The boy was about my age, but everything about him made me uneasy – especially the fact that my father gave him to me as a present.

"I don't like him," I said. "I'd rather have a puppy."

A violent fit of coughing seized my father. It took him a few moments to recover.

"Don't be stupid. He's worth a lot more than a dog. If I hadn't seen him with my own eyes, I would never have believed he's real." His voice grew ethereal as he went on.

A susurrating noise grew louder. I shuddered; the typhoon was here.

The wind blew the boy's scent to me, a strong, briny stench that reminded me of a fish, a common, slender, iron-black, cheap fish trawled from the ocean.

*That's a good name for him, isn't it?* I thought.

#

My father had long planned out everything about my life up through age forty-five.

At eighteen I would attend a college right here in Guangdong Province and study business – the school couldn't be more than three hours from home by train.

In college, I would not be allowed to date. This was because my father had already picked out a girl for me: the daughter of his business partner Lao Luo. Indeed, he had taken the trouble to go to a fortuneteller to ensure that the eight characters of our birth times were compatible.

After graduation, Lao Luo's daughter and I would get married. By my twenty-fifth year, my father would have his first grandchild. By twenty-eight I would give him another. And depending on the sexes of the first two, he might want a third as well.

Simultaneous with the birth of my first child, I would also join the family business. He would take me around to pay my respects to all his partners and suppliers (he had gotten to know most of them in the army).

Since I was expected to work very long hours, who would take care of my child? His mother, of course – see, my father already decided it would be a boy. My wife would stay home; there would be two sets of grandparents; and we could hire nannies.

By age thirty I would take over the Lin Family Tea Company. In the five years prior to this point, I would have to to master all aspects of the tea trade, from identification of tea leaves to manufacture and transport, as well as the strengths and weaknesses of all my father's partners and competitors.

For the next fifteen years, with my retired father as my advisor, I would lead the family business to new heights: branching out into other provinces and spreading Lin tea leafs all over China, and if I'm lucky, perhaps even breaking into the overseas trade, a lifelong goal that my father had always wanted – but also hesitated – to pursue.

By the time I was forty-five, my oldest child would be close to graduating from college. At that point, I would follow in my father's footsteps and find a good wife for him.

Everything in my father's universe functioned as an essential component in an intricate piece of well-maintained clockwork: gear meshed with gear, wheel turned upon wheel, motion without end.

Whenever I argued with him over his grand plan for me, he always brought up my grandfather, his grandfather, and then my grandfather's grandfather – he would point at the wall of ancestors' portraits and denounce me for forgetting my roots.

*This is the way the Lin family has survived*, he would say. *Are you telling me you are no longer a Lin?*

Sometimes I wondered if I was really living in the twenty-first century.

#

I called him Balin. In our topolect, *balin* meant a fish with scales.

In reality, he looked more like a goat, especially when he lifted his eyes to gaze at the horizon, his two hair buns poking up like horns. My father told me that the *paoxiao* have an incredibly strong sense of direction. Even if they were blindfolded, hogtied, tossed into the dark hold of a ship, hauled across the ocean on a journey lasting weeks, and sold and resold through numerous buyers, they'd still be able to find their way home. Of course, given the geopolitical disputes in the South China Sea, exactly what country was their home was indeterminate.

"Then do we need to leash him like a dog?" I asked my father.

He chuckled unnaturally. "The *paoxiao* are even more accepting of fate than we. They believe everything that happens to them is by the will of the gods and spirits; that's why they'll never run away."

Gradually, Balin grew used to his new environment. My father repurposed our old chicken coop as his home. It took him a long time to figure out that the bedding was meant for him to sleep on, but even after that, he preferred to sleep on the rough, sandy floor. He ate just about everything, even crunching the chicken bones leftover after our meals. I and the other children of the village enjoyed crouching outside his hutch to watch him eat. This was also the only time when I could see his teeth clearly: densely packed, sharp triangles like the teeth of a shark; they easily ripped apart whatever he stuffed into his mouth.

As I watched, I couldn't help imagining the feeling of those sharp teeth tearing into me; I would then shudder with a complicated sensation, a mixture of pain and addictive pleasure.

One day, after Balin had eaten enough, he leisurely crawled out of his enclosure. His thin figure sporting a bulging, round tummy resembled a twig with a swelling gall. A couple of other kids and I were playing "monster in the water." Balin, waddling from side to side, stopped not far from us and watched our game with curiosity.

"Shrimp! Shrimp! Watch out if you don't want one to bite off your toes!" Shouting and screaming, we pretended to be fishermen standing on shore (a short brick wall) gingerly sticking our feet into the (nonexistent) river. Dip. Dip. Pull back.

The boy who was the water monster ran back and forth, trying to grab the bare feet of the fishermen as they dipped into the river. Only by pulling a fisherman into the river would the water monster be redeemed to humanity, and his unlucky victim would turn into the new water monster.

No one remembered when Balin joined our game. But then Nana, a neighbor, abruptly stopped and pointed. I looked and saw Balin imitating the movements of the water monster: leaping over here, bounding over there. Except that he wasn't grabbing or snatching at the feet of fishermen, but empty air.

Children often liked to imitate the speech or body language of others, but what Balin was doing was unlike anything I had ever seen. Balin's movements were almost in perfect synchrony with Ah Hui, the boy who was the water monster.

I say "almost" because it was impossible to detect with the naked eye whether there was a delay between Balin's movements and Ah Hui's. Balin was like a shadow that Ah Hui had cast five meters away. Each time Ah Hui turned, each time he extended his hand, even each time he paused dispiritedly because he had missed a fisherman – every gesture was mirrored by Balin perfectly.

I couldn't understand how Balin was accomplishing this feat, as though he was moving without thinking.

Finally, Ah Hui stopped because everyone was staring.

Ah Hui took a few steps toward Balin; Balin took a few steps toward Ah Hui. Even the way they dragged their heels was exactly the same.

"Why are you copying me?" demanded Ah Hui.

Balin's lips moved in synchrony, though the syllables that emerged from his mouth were mere noise, like the screeching of a broken radio.

Ah Hui pushed Balin, but he stumbled back because Balin also pushed him at the same moment.

The crowd of children grew excited at the farcical scene, far more interesting than the water monster game.

"Fight! Fight!"

Ah Hui jump at Balin, and the two grappled with each other. This was a fascinating fight because their motions mirrored each other exactly. Soon, neither could move as they were locked in a stalemate, staring into each other's eyes.

"That's enough! Go home, all of you!" Massive hands picked both of them off the ground and forcibly separated them as though parting a pair of conjoined twins. It was Father.

Ah Hui angrily spat on the ground. The children scattered.

Balin did not imitate Ah Hui this time. It was as though some switch had been shut off in him.

Smiling, Father glanced at me, as though to say, *Now do you understand why this present is so great?*

#

"We can view the human brain as a machine with just three functions: sensing, thinking, and motor control. If we use a computer as an analogy, sensing is the input, thinking is the computation carried out by the switches, and motor control is the output – the brain's only means of interacting with the external world. Do you see why?"

Before knowing Mr. Lu, I would never have believed that a gym teacher would give this sort of speech.

Mr. Lu was a local legend. He was not that tall, only about five-foot-eight, his hair cropped short. Through the thin shirts he wore in summers we could see his bulging muscles. It was said that he had studied abroad.

Everyone in our class was puzzled why somebody who had left China and seen the world would want to return to our tiny, poor town to be a middle school teacher. Later, we heard that Mr. Lu was an only child. His father was bedridden with a chronic illness, and his mother had died early. Since there were no other relatives who could care for his father and the old man refused to leave town, saying that he preferred to die where he was born, Mr. Lu had no choice but to move home and find a teaching job. Since his degree was in the neurology of motor control, the principal naturally thought he would be qualified to teach phys ed.

Unlike our other teachers, Mr. Lu never put on any airs around us. He joked about with us as though we were all friends.

Once, I asked him, "Why did you come back to this town?"

"There's an old Confucian saying that as long as your parents are alive, you should not travel too far. I'd been far away from home for more than a decade, and my father won't be with me for much longer. I have to think about him."

I asked him another question: "Will you leave after both your parents are gone then?"

Mr. Lu frowned, as though he didn't want to think about the question. Then he said, "In my field there was a pioneering researcher named Donald Broadbent. He once said that it was far harder to control human behavior than to control the stimuli influencing them. That was why in the study of motor control it was difficult to devise simple scientific laws of the form 'A leads to B'."

"So?" I asked, knowing that he had no intention of answering my question.

"So no one knows what will happen in the future." He nodded and took a long drag of his cigarette.

"Bullshit," I said, accepting the cigarette from him and taking a puff.

No one thought he would stick around our town for long.

In the end he was my gym teacher from eighth grade through twelfth grade, married a local woman, and had kids.

Just the way he predicted.

#

At first we used a push pin, and then we switched to the electric igniter for a cigarette lighter. *Snap!* There it was: a pale blue electric arc.

Father thought this was more civilized.

The people who had sold Balin to him had also taught him a trick. If he wanted Balin to imitate someone, he should have Balin face the target and lock gazes. Then he should "stimulate" Balin in some way. Once Balin's eyes glazed over then the "connection" was established. They explained to my father that this was a unique custom of Balin's kind.

Balin brought us endless entertainment.

As long as I could remember, I'd always enjoyed street puppetry, whether shadow puppets, glove puppets, or marionettes. Curious, I would sneak behind the stage and watch the performers give life to the inanimate and enact moving scenes of love and revenge. In my child-hood, such transformations had seemed magical, and now with Balin, I finally had the chance to practice my own brand of magic.

I danced, and so did he. I boxed, and so did he. I had been shy about putting on a performance in front of my relatives, but now, through Balin's body, I became the family entertainer.

I had Balin imitate Father when he was drunk. I had him imitate anyone who was different in town: the madman, the cripple, the idiot, the beggar who had broken legs and arms and who had to crawl along the ground like a worm, the epileptic... my friends and I would laugh so hard that we would roll on the ground – until the relatives of our victims came after us, wielding bamboo laundry rods.

Balin was also good at imitating animals: he was best at cats, dogs, oxen, goats, pigs; not so good with ducks and chickens; and completely useless when it came to fish.

Sometimes, I found him crouched outside the door to the main house in the ancestral compound spying on our TV. He was especially fascinated by animal documentaries. When he saw prey being hunted down and killed by predators, Balin's body twitched and spasmed uncon-trollably, as though he was the one whose belly was being ripped open, his entrails spilling forth.

There were times when Balin grew tired. While imitating a target, his movements would slow and diverge from the target's, like a wind-up figurine running down or a toy car with almost-exhausted batteries. Af-ter a while, he would fall to the ground and stop moving, and no matter how hard we kicked him, he refused to budge. The only solution was to make him eat, stuff him to the gills.

Other than exhaustion, he never resisted or showed any signs of unhappiness. In my childish eyes, Balin was no different from the puppets constructed from hide, cellophane, fabric, or wood. He was nothing more than an object faithfully carrying out the controller's will, but he himself was devoid of emotion. His imitation was nothing more than an unthinking reflex.

Eventually, we tired of controlling Balin one-on-one, and we invented more complex and also crueler multiplayer games.

First, we decided the order through rock-paper-scissors. The winner got to control Balin to fight against the loser. The winner of the contest then got to fight against the next kid in line. I was the first.

The experience was cool beyond measure. Like a general sitting safe far from the frontlines, I commanded my soldier on the battlefield to press, punch, dodge, kick, roundhouse... because I was at a distance from the fight, I could discern my opponent's intentions and movements with more clarity, and devise better attacks and responses. Moreover, since Balin was the one who endured all the pain, I had no fear and could attack ruthlessly.

I thought my victory was certain.

But for some reason, all my carefully planned moves, as they were carried out by Balin, seemed to lack strength. Even punches and kicks that landed squarely against my opponent did little to shock, much less to injure. Soon, Balin was on the ground, enduring a hailstorm of punches.

"Bite him! Bite!" I snapped my jaw in the air, knowing the power of

Illustration by Wang Yan

Balin's sharp teeth.

But Balin was like a marionette whose strings had been cut. My opponent's fists did not relent, and soon Balin's cheeks were swollen.

"Dammit!" I spat on the ground, conceding the fight.

Now it was my turn to face Balin, controlled by the victor of the last round. I stared at him as ferociously as I could manage. His face was bloody, the skin around his eyes bruised and puffy, but his irises still held their habitual tranquility. I was enraged.

Glancing out the corner of my eye, I observed the movements of Ah Hui, Balin's controller. I was familiar with how Ah Hui fought. He always stepped forward with his left foot and punched with his right fist. I was going to surprise him with a low spinning sweep kick to knock him off his feet. Once he was on the ground, the fight would basically be over.

Ah Hui stepped forward with his left foot. *Here it comes.* I was about to crouch down and begin my sweep, but Balin's foot moved and kicked up the dirt at his feet, blinding me in an instant. Next, his leg swept low along the ground, and I was the one knocked off my feet. My eyes squeezed shut, I wrapped my arms about my head, preparing to endure a fusillade of punches.

However, the fight did not proceed the way I imagined. The punches did land against my body, but there was no force behind them at all. At first, I thought Balin was probably tired, but soon realized that was not the case. Ah Hui's own punches against the air were forceful and precise, but Balin apparently was holding back on purpose so that his punches landed on my body like caresses.

Without warning, the punching stopped. Something warm and smelly pressed itself against my face.

Laughter erupted around me. When I finally understood what had happened, a wave of heat suffused my face.

Balin had sat on me with his nude and dirty bottom.

Ah Hui knew that Balin's punches were useless, which was why he had come up with such a dirty trick.

I pushed Balin away and leapt up off the ground. In one quick motion, I pressed Balin to the ground and held him down. Tears poured out of my eyes, stung by the kicked-up sand as well as humiliation and rage. Balin looked up at me, his swollen eyes also filled with tears, as though he knew exactly how I felt at that moment.

Then it hit me. *He's just imitating.* I raised my fist.

"Why didn't you punch with real force, like I wanted you to?"

My fist pounded against Balin's thin body, thumping as though I was punching a hollow shell made of fragile plywood.

"Why don't you hit me back?"

My fingers felt the teeth beneath his lips rattling.

"Tell me why!"

A crisp *snap* of bone. A wound opened over Balin's right brow, the torn skin extended to the tip of his eye. Pink and white fascia and fat spilled out from under the dark skin, and bright red blood flowed freely, soon pooling on the sandy earth under him.

A heavy, fish-like scent wafted from his body.

Terrified, I got off him and stepped back. The other children were stunned as well.

The dust settled, and Balin lay still, curled up like a slaughtered lamb. He glanced at me with his left eye, the one not covered in blood. The tranquil orb still betrayed no emotion. In that moment, for the first time, I felt that he was like me: he was made of flesh and blood; he was a person with a soul.

The moment lasted only seconds. Almost instinctively, I realized that if I had not been treating Balin as a human being until this moment, then it was impossible for me to do so in the future either.

I brushed off the dirt on my pants and shoved my way through the crowd of children, never looking back.

# Chen Qiufan

#

I enter "Ghost" mode, experiencing everything experienced by Balin, trapped in his VR suit.

I – Balin – we are standing on some beautiful tropical island. Based on my suggestion, the environment artist has combined the sights and vegetation from multiple South China Sea islands to create this reality. Even the angle and temperature of light are calculated to be accurate for the latitude.

My intent is to give Balin the sensation of being back home – his real home. But the environment doesn't seem to have reduced his terror.

The view whirls violently: sky, sand, the ocean nearby, scattered vines, and from time to time, even rough gray polygonal structures whose textures have yet to be applied.

I feel dizzy. This is the result of visual signals and bodily motion being out of sync. The eyes tell my brain that I'm moving, but the vestibular system tells my brain that I'm not. The conflict between the two sets of signals gives rise to a feeling of sickness.

For Balin, we have deployed the most advanced techniques to shrink the signal delay to within five milliseconds. In addition, we are using motion capture technology to synchronize the movements between his virtual body and his physical body. He could move freely on the omnidirectional treadmill, but his position wouldn't shift one inch.

We're treating him like a guest in first class, anticipating all his needs.

Balin stands rooted to his spot. He can't understand how the world in his eyes is related to the bright, sterile lab he was in just a few minutes ago.

"This is useless," I bark at the technicians through my microphone. "We've got to get him to move!"

Balin's head whips around. The surround sound system in his helmet warns him of movements behind his body. A quaking wave ripples through the dense jungle, and a flock of birds erupts into the air. Something gigantic is shoving its way through the vegetation, making its way toward Balin. Motionless, Balin stares at the bush.

A massive herd of prehistoric creatures bursts from the jungle. Even I, no expert on evolutionary biology, can tell that they don't belong to the same geologic epoch. The technicians have used whatever models they can find in the database to try to get Balin to move.

Still, he stands there like a tree stump, enduring waves of Tyrannosaurus rexes, saber-toothed tigers, monstrous dragonflies, crocodilian-shaped ancestors of dinosaurs, and strange arthropods as they rush at him and then, howling and screaming, sweep through him like wisps of mist. This is a bug in the physics engine, but if we were to fix the bug and fully simulate the physical experience, the VR user would not be able to endure the impact.

It isn't over yet.

The ground under Balin begins to quake and split. Trees lean over and topple. Volcanoes erupt and crimson molten lava spills out of the earth, coalescing into bloody rivers. Massive waves more than ten meters tall charge at our position from the sea.

"I think you might be overdoing this a bit," I say into the mic. I hear faint giggles.

Imagine how a primitive human tossed into the middle of such an apocalyptic scene would feel. Would he consider himself a savior who is suffering for the sins of the entire human race? Or would he be on the cusp of madness, his senses on the verge of collapse?

Or would he behave like Balin: no reaction at all?

Suddenly, I understand the truth.

I back out of Ghost mode, and remove Balin's helmet. Sensors are studded like pearls all over his skull. His eyes are squeezed tightly shut, the wrinkles around them so deep that they resemble insect antennae.

"Let's stop here today." I sigh helplessly, recalling that afternoon long ago when I had punched him until he bled.

#

As the time approached for all the high school students to declare our intended subjects of study before the college entrance examination, the war between my father and me heated up.

According to his grand plan, I was supposed to major in political science or history in college, but I had zero interest in those subjects, which I viewed as painted whores at the whim of those in power. I wanted to major in a hard science like physics, or at the minimum biology – something that according to Mr. Lu involved "fundamental questions."

My father was contemptuous of my reasons. He pointed to the houses in our ancestral compound, and the tea leaves drying over the racks in the yard, glistening like gold dust in the bright sunlight.

"Do you think there are any questions more fundamental than making a living and feeding your family?"

It was like discussing music theory with a cud-chewing cow.

I gave up trying to convince Father. I had my own plan. With Mr. Lu's help, I obtained permission from the teachers to cram for common subjects like math, Chinese, and English with students who intended to declare for the humanities, but then I would sneak away to study physics, chemistry, and biology with the science students. If class schedules conflicted, I would make my own choices and then make up the missed work later.

My teachers were willing to let me get away with it because they had their own selfish hopes. Rather than forcing someone who had no interest to study politics and history, they thought they might as well let me follow my heart. If they got lucky, it was possible that I would do extraordinarily well on the college entrance examination as a science student and bring honor to them all.

I thought my plan would fool my busy father, who was away from home more often than not. I was going to surprise him at the last minute, when I had to fill out the desired majors and top choice schools right before the examination. Even if he blew up at me then, it would be too late.

I was so naive.

On the day we were supposed to fill out the forms, all my friends received a copy of the blank form except me. I thought the head teacher had made a mistake.

"Uh… your father already filled it out for you." The teacher dared not meet my eyes.

I don't remember how I made it home that day. Like a lost, homeless dog, I wandered the streets and alleyways of the town aimlessly until I found myself in front of the ancestral compound.

Father was entertaining himself by playing with Balin. He had dug up an old set of army uniforms and put them on Balin. The loose folds and wide pant legs hung on Balin like a tent, making him resemble a monkey who had stolen some human clothing. Father had Balin follow orders he had learned during the time he was in the army: stand at attention, stand at ease, right dress, left dress, march in place, and so on. When I was in elementary school, Father had enjoyed ordering me around like a drill sergeant at the parade ground, and I had hated those "games" more than anything else.

It had been years since he had tried anything like that with me, but now he had found a new recruit.

A soldier who would obey every one of his commands without question.

"One-two-one! One-two-one! Forwaaaaard-march!" As he barked out the commands and demonstrated the moves, Balin goose-stepped around the yard, his pant legs muddy as they dragged on the ground.

I stepped between them and faced my father. "You have no intention of letting me go to college, is that it?"

"Riiiiight-dress!" My father whipped his head to the right and shuffled his feet. I heard the sound of feet scrabbling against the ground in synchrony behind me.

"You knew about my plan a long time ago, didn't you?" I demanded.

"But you said nothing before you played your trick so I wouldn't have a chance to stop you."

"Maaaaarch in place!"

Enraged, I turned around and held Balin still, not allowing him to proceed any longer like a mindless drone. But he seemed unable to stop. The pant legs slapped against the ground, whipping up wisps of dust.

I grabbed his head and forced him to lock gazes with me. I pulled out the electric lighter from my pocket and flicked it; a pale blue arc burst into life next to his temple. Balin screamed like a baby.

I looked into his eyes; now he belonged to me.

"You have no right to control me! All you care about is your business. Have you ever thought about what I want for my future?"

As I screamed at my father, Balin marched around us, his finger also pointing at Father, his mouth also screaming. The circle he made around the two of us tightened on each loop.

"I'm going to college whether you want me to go or not. And I'm going to study whatever I want!" I clenched my jaw. Balin's finger was almost touching my father. "Let me tell you something, Father: I *never* want to become like you."

The militaristic arrogance melted from my father. He stood there, his face fallen and back hunched, like crops that had been bitten by frost. I expected him to hit back, hard, as was his wont, but he did not.

"I knew. I've always known that you don't want to walk the path others have paved for you." My father's voice faded until it was barely a whisper. "You remind me so much of myself when I was your age. But I have no choice—"

"So you want me to repeat your life?"

My father's knees buckled. I thought he was going to fall, but he knelt on the ground and embraced Balin.

"You can't leave!" he shouted. "I know what's going to happen if you go away to college. No one who leaves this town ever returns."

I struggled against the empty air so that Balin, moving in sync with me, could free himself from my father's grasp. As long as I could remember, my father had never hugged me.

"Don't be so childish! Open your eyes! See the world for what it is."

Balin was like a wind-up toy that had malfunctioned. His limbs whipped about in a frenzy; the military uniform he wore was torn in multiple places, revealing the dark, unreflective skin.

"The way you spoke just now is just like your mother." Another pale blue spark came to life over Balin's temple. Abruptly, he ceased struggling, and held my father tightly like a long-lost lover. "Are you going to abandon me just like she did?"

I was stunned.

I had never thought about this matter from my father's perspective. I had always thought that he wanted to keep me close at hand because he was selfish, narrow-minded, but I had never seen it as a reaction to the fear of being abandoned. My mother had left us when I was too young to view it as trauma, but it cast a shadow over the rest of his life.

Wordless, I approached my father, who held on to Balin tightly. I bent down and caressed his spine, no longer as straight as in my memory. Maybe this was as close as the two of us would ever be.

I saw the tears spilling from the corners of Balin's eyes. For a moment, I doubted myself.

*Maybe it isn't just about control and power, but also love.*

#

There are many things I wish I had known before I turned seventeen.

For example, the fact that most of the structures in the human brain have something to do with motor functions, including the cerebellum, the basal ganglia, the brainstem, the motor region of the cerebral cortex and the direct projection of the somatosensory cortex to the primary motor cortex, and so on.

For example, the cerebellum contains more neurons than any other part of the brain. As humans evolved, the cerebellar cortex grew in step with the rapidly increasing volume of the frontal lobe.

For example, any interaction with the outside world, whether informational or physical, including moving limbs, manipulating tools, gesticulating, speaking, glancing, making faces – each ultimately requires activating a series of muscles to realize.

For example, an arm contains twenty-six separate muscles, and each muscle on average contains a hundred motor units, each made up by a motor neuron and its associated skeletal muscle fibers. Thus, the motion of a single arm is governed by a possibility space at least $2^{2600}$ in size, a number far greater than the total number of atoms in the universe.

Human motion is so complex and subtle, and each casual movement represents the result of so much computation, analysis, and planning that even the most advanced robots are incapable of moving as well as a three-year-old.

And we haven't even discussed all the information, emotion, and culture embodied in human motion.

On the way to the high-speed rail station, my father maintained his silence, only clutching my suitcase tightly. The northbound train finally appeared before us, shiny, new, smooth in outline, like something that was going to slide into the unknowable future the moment the brakes were released.

In the end, my father and I failed to reach a compromise. If I was going to college in Beijing, he would not pay for any of my expenses.

"Unless you promise to return," he said.

I gazed through him, as though I was already seeing the future, a future that belonged to me. For that, I was willing to be the black sheep from a white flock, the sheep in perpetual exile.

"Dad, take care of yourself."

I grabbed my suitcase to board the train, but my father refused to let go of the handle, and the suitcase awkwardly hung between us. A moment later, both of us let go, and the suitcase fell to the ground.

I was about to erupt when my father slapped his heels together to stand at attention, giving me a crisp military salute. Without a word, he turned and left. He had once told me that it was bad luck to say goodbye before going to war. Better to leave each other with other memories.

I watched his diminishing figure, raised my hand, and returned his salute gently.

I did not truly understand the meaning in my gesture.

#

"I never thought we'd fail because of a wild man," says my thesis advisor Ouyang, who is also the project leader. He claps me on the shoulder, his smile disguising the sharp edges of his words. "It's no big deal. Let's keep on working at this. We still have time."

But I know him too well. What he really means is, *We are running out of time.*

Or, to put it another way, *This is your idea, your project. Whether you can get your degree in time will depend on what you do next.*

Of course he will never mention how much of our time he has taken up in the past to handle the random projects he promised business investors.

Frustrated, I massage my scalp. My eyes fall on Balin, now shut in his pink-hued pet enclosure. Eyes glazed, he stares at the floor, as though still not recovered from his ordeal in the VR environment. The contrast between the pink pet enclosure and his appearance is comical, but I can't make myself laugh.

*What would Mr. Lu do?*

Everything began with that idle conversation with him years ago concerning "A leads to B."

Traditional theorists believe that motor control is the result of stored programs. When a person wants to move a certain way, the motor cortex picks out a certain program from its stored repertoire and carries it out much the same way a player piano follows the roll of perforated paper. The program's instructions determine the activation patterns in the motor regions of the cortex and the spinal cord, which then, in turn, activate the muscles to complete the motion.

This naturally raises the question: the same motion can be carried out in infinite ways. How does the brain store an infinite number of motor programs?

Remember that arm whose potential possible number of movements exceeds the number of atoms in the universe?

In 2002, the mathematician Emanuel Todorov came up with a theory in an attempt to answer this question. Basically, he argued that motor control is really an optimization problem for the brain. Optimality is defined by high-level performance criteria such as maximizing precision, minimizing energy consumption, minimizing control effort, and so on.

In the optimization process, the brain relies on the processing powers of the cerebellum. Before the commands for movement have reached muscles, the cerebellum predicts the results of anticipated motion, and then, combined with real-time sensory feedback, helps the brain evaluate and coordinate the motor commands.

A simple example: when ascending or descending a set of stairs, we will often stumble due to miscounting the number of steps. If feedback-based adjustments are made in time, we can recover and not fall. Feedback, of course, is often noisy and involves a delay.

Todorov's mathematical model is consistent with all known evidence concerning the neural mechanisms of motor control and can be used to explain all kinds of behavioral phenomena. Given some physical parameters, it's even possible to predict the resulting motion using his model:

for instance, how an eight-legged creature would jump in Pluto's gravity.

Physics engines based on his models are used by Hollywood to produce naturalistic movements for avatars in virtual environments.

By the time I was in college, the Todorov model was already treated as textbook authority. Experiment after experiment provided more evidence that it was correct.

And then one day, Mr. Lu and I discussed Balin.

After I left home for college, he and I had kept in touch via email. He was like an oracular AI from whom I could get answers for everything: academics, awkward social situations, even relationship advice. We wrote long emails back and forth discussing questions that must have seemed ridiculous to anyone else, such as "would an out-of-body experience engineered by technology violate religion's claim on spirituality?"

By an unspoken agreement, both of us avoided talking about my father.

Mr. Lu told me that Balin had been sold to another family in town, a nouveau riche household which was often mocked for conspicuous acts of consumption that appeared ridiculous in the townspeople's eyes.

I had known that Father's business had run into a rough patch, but I hadn't imagined that he would be so short on cash as to consider selling Balin.

I shifted the topic to the Todorov mathematical model, and a new thought struck me. Balin was capable of imitating movements with perfect precision. Suppose we had him perform two sets of identical movements: one through subconscious imitation and the other by his own will; do these two sets of movements go through the same process of motor control?

Mathematically, there was only a single optimal solution, but was there a difference in the way the optimal solution was arrived at?

It took Mr. Lu three days to get back to me. Unlike his usual free-flowing, loquacious style, this time he wrote only a few lines:

*I think you're asking a very important question, one whose importance perhaps you don't even realize. If we can't distinguish between mechanical imitation and conscious, willed movement at the level of neural activity, then the question is: Does free will truly exist?*

I couldn't sleep that night. I spent two weeks designing the prototype experiment, and spent even more time studying the feasibility of my proposed study, soliciting feedback from my mentors and other professors. Then I submitted my project for approval.

It wasn't until everything was ready that I realized that this experiment, one seeking to address a "fundamental question," lacked a fundamental, required component.

I had no choice but to break my promise to myself and go home.

*I'm going just to get Balin,* I reminded myself again and again. *Just for Balin.*

Just like how A leads to B. Simple, right?

#

I once read a science fiction novel called *The Orphans*, which was about aliens who had come to Earth. They could imitate the appearance of specific humans and pass as human in society, but they couldn't perfectly capture the characteristic ways their targets moved or the subtleties of their facial expressions. Many aliens, exposed as frauds, were hunted down by humans.

In order to survive, the aliens had to study how humans communicated via body language. They pretended to be abandoned orphans, and, once taken in by kind-hearted families, proceeded to use the opportunity of living together to imitate the mannerisms and expressions of their adoptive parents.

To the parents' surprise, their children became more and more like them. And once the alien orphans decided that they had learned enough, they killed their father or mother, took on their appearance, and took their place. The scene where an alien killed his father and took his mother as his wife was unforgettable.

Though it became harder to tell aliens apart from humans, people finally discovered the fundamental difference between the extraterrestrials and humans.

Although the aliens were able to imitate human movements with perfect fidelity, they lacked the mirror neurons unique to human brains, and thus were unable to intuit the emotional shifts occurring behind human faces or to experience similar neural activation patterns in their own minds. In other words, they lacked the capacity for empathy.

And so humans devised an effective means to detect aliens: bring harm to those closest to the disguised aliens and observe the aliens for signs of pain, fear, or rage. The test was called "the stabbing needle test."

The story's lesson seems to be: humanity isn't the only species in the universe that has difficulty relating to their parents.

#

Mr. Lu knew everything about Balin. He thought of the *paoxiao* as an example of overdevelopment in the mirror neuron system. He was fascinated by Balin, but he disapproved of the way we treated him.

"But he's never resisted or even wanted to run away," I used to counter.

"Overactive mirror neurons lead to a pathological excess of empathy," he said. "Maybe he just couldn't tolerate the look of abandonment in his tormentors' – your – eyes."

"I guess that could be true," I said. "I must be an example of underdevelopment of mirror neurons."

"Cold-blooded, one might say."

But when Mr. Lu took me to find Balin on my return, I realized that I wasn't the most cold-blooded, not by far.

Balin was naked, his body covered in bruises and lacerations. Thick, rusty chains were locked about his neck and shackled his arms and legs. He was shut inside a tiny brick-and-mud enclosure, about five feet on each side. The interior was dim, and the stale air saturated with the gag-inducing stench of excrement and rotting food. He was thinner than I remembered. Flies buzzed about his wounds, and the outlines of his skeleton poked from under his skin. He was like an animal about to be sent to the butcher's.

He looked at me, and there was no reaction in his eyes at all. It was just like the first time we had met, that summer night when I was thirteen.

"They had him mirror the movements of animals... mating—" Mr. Lu was unable to continue.

Memories of the past flood into my mind in a flash.

I have no recollection of what happened next. It was as though I had been possessed by some spirit, and I moved without remembering wanting to move.

According to Mr. Lu, I rushed into the house of Balin's new owners, and grabbed the Pomeranian beloved by the family patriarch's daughter-in-law. I opened my jaw and held the neck of the whimpering creature between my teeth.

"You said, 'If you don't let Balin go, I'm going to bite all the way through,'" Mr. Lu said.

I spat on the ground. Though I didn't remember any of it, this did sound like something I would do.

Mr. Lu and I rushed Balin to the hospital. As we were preparing to leave, Mr. Lu stopped me. "Do you want to see your father?"

That was how I found out that my father had been hospitalized. Once in college, I had had almost no contact with him, and gradually, I had stopped even thinking about him.

He looked about ten years older. Tubing was stuck into his nostrils and arms. His hair was sparse, and his gaze unsteady. A few years ago, when Pu'er tea was all the rage, he had gambled with all his chips and ended up as the last fool to buy in at the height of the mania. He was stuck with warehouses full of tea leaves as the price collapsed, and ended up losing just about everything.

As he looked at me, I noted that his expression reminded me of Balin, as though he was saying, *I knew you'd be back.*

"I... I'm here for Balin," I said.

My father saw through my façade and cracked a smile, revealing a mouthful of teeth stained yellow by years of smoking.

"That little gremlin? He's much smarter than you think. We all thought we were controlling him, but sometimes I wonder if he was controlling all of us."

I didn't know what to say.

"It's the same way with you. I always thought I was the one in charge. But after you left, I realized that you had always held a thread whose other end is looped around my heart. No matter how far away you are, as soon as you twitch your fingers, I suffer pangs of heartache." My father closed his eyes and put his hand over his chest.

Something was stuck in my throat.

I walked up to his bed and wanted to lean down to embrace him. But halfway through the motion, my body refused to obey. Awkwardly, I clapped him on the shoulder, straightened up, and walked away.

"I'm glad you're back," my father said from behind me, his voice hoarse. I didn't turn around.

Mr. Lu was waiting for me at the door. I pretended to scratch my eyes to disguise the emotional turmoil.

"Do you think fate likes to play jokes on us?" he asked.

"What do you mean?"

"You wanted to escape the route your father had paved for you, but in the end, you ended up in the same place as me."

"I think I'm coming around to your way of thinking."

"What's that?" he asked.

"No one knows what will happen in the future."

#

We've failed again.

The original premise is very simple: Balin's hypertrophic mirror neuron system makes him the ideal experimental subject because his imitation is a kind of instinct. Thus, his movements during imitation ought to be free from much of the noise and interference found in human motor control due to conscious cognition.

We use non-invasive electrodes to capture the neural activity in Balin's motor cortex as he's imitating a sequence of movements. Then we have him repeat the sequence under his own will and use motion capture to ensure that we get a perfect match between the two sets of movements. Mathematically, that means that the two sequences are indistinguishable; they are the same motion.

Then, by comparing the two sets of neural patterns captured during the process, we can find out if the same neural signals were activating the same regions of the motor cortex in the same sequence and with the same strength.

If there are differences, then the Todorov model, accepted as gospel, will have been revealed to be seriously lacking.

But if there are no differences, the consequences will be even more severe. Maybe human beings are doing nothing but imitating the behaviors of other individuals, and are only operating under the illusion of free will.

No matter what, the result of the experiment ought to be earth-shattering.

Yet, the experiment was a failure from the very beginning. Balin has refused to look into anyone's eyes, and has refused to imitate anyone's movements, including me.

I can guess the reason, but I have no solution. My team has vowed to solve the secret of human cognition, yet we can't even heal the psychic trauma inflicted on a mere "primitive."

I thought of the idea of using virtual reality. Situating Balin in an environment completely disconnected from the reality around him may help him recover his normal habits.

And so we went through a series of virtual environments: islands, glaciers, deserts, even space; we manufactured incredible catastrophes; we even devoted enormous effort to construct avatars of *paoxiao*, hoping that the sight of others of his kind would awaken his dormant mirror neurons.

Without exception, all these tricks have failed.

Now, at midnight, only I and the zombie-like Balin remain in the lab. Everyone else has left. I know what they're thinking: this experiment is a joke, and I'm the man who has finished telling the joke and looks around confused, unsure why everyone else is laughing.

Balin is curled up into a ball in the pet house made from pink foam boards. I remember Mr. Lu's words. He was right. I've never treated Balin as a person, not even now.

A colleague once implanted a wireless receiver into a rat's brain. By electrically stimulating the rat's somatosensory cortex and the medial forebrain bundle, my colleague was able to induce sensations of pleasure and pain in the rat, thereby controlling where the rat moved.

There's no qualitative difference between that and what I'm doing to Balin.

I am indeed a bastard whose mirror neurons are atrophied.

Unbidden, the memory of a children's game resurfaces, the game in which Balin first showed us his fantastic ability.

"Shrimp! Shrimp! Watch out if you don't want one to bite off your toes!"

I chant in a low voice, embarrassed. I pretend to be a fisherman, dipping my foot into the imaginary river from the shore and quickly pulling back.

Balin glances at me.

"Shrimp! Shrimp! Watch out if you don't want one to bite off your toes!" My chant grows louder.

Balin stares at my clumsy movements. Gently, slowly, he crawls out of the pet house, stopping a few steps away from me.

"Shrimp! Shrimp! Watch out if you don't want one to bite off your toes!" My legs are jerking wildly like some caricature of a pole dancer in a club.

Abruptly, Balin jumps at me with incredible speed, moving the exact way Ah Hui used to.

He remembers; he remembers everything.

Balin leaps and bounds, grabbing at my dipping leg. A baby-like gurgle emerges from his throat. He's laughing. This is the first time I've ever heard him laugh in the all the years I've known him.

He is now re-enacting the movements of everyone in town who had been a bit different. All their movements seem to have been engraved in Balin's brain, so vivid and precise that I can recognize who he's replaying at a glance. In turn, he becomes the madman, the cripple, the idiot, the beggar who had broken legs and arms, and the epileptic; he is a cat, a dog, an ox, a goat, a pig, and a crude chicken; he is my drunk father and me, dancing about in joy.

In a moment, I've traveled through thousands of kilometers and returned to the hometown of my childhood.

Without warning, Balin begins to play two roles simultaneously, reenacting the day of the rupture between me and my father.

Watching the argument between me and my father as an observer is eerie: the movements before me are so familiar, yet my memories have grown indistinct, unreal. I was so angry then, so stubborn, like a wild horse that refused to accept the bit. My father, on the other hand, was so pitiful and meek. Again and again, he backed off; he suffered. It is nothing like how I remember the scene.

Balin quickly switches between roles, gesturing and posturing like a skilled mime.

Though I know what happens next, when it does happen I'm not prepared.

Balin wraps his arms about me, just the way my father back then wrapped his arms about him. He hugs me tightly, his head buried in the crook of my neck. I smell that familiar fish-like scent, like the sea, and a warm liquid flows down my collar like a river that has absorbed the heat of the sun.

I stay still, thinking about how to react.

Then I give up thinking, allowing my body to react and open up, hugging him back the way I would hug an old friend, the way I would hug my father.

I know that I have owed this hug for far too long, to him and to my father.

I think I finally understand how to solve the problem.

#

At the end of *The Orphans*, the team that had come up with the stabbing needle test found, to their horror, that even when they harmed the aliens passing as human, their dear ones, the real humans, also failed to react. Their mirror neuron systems would not activate.

Humanity is a species that was never designed to truly empathize with another species.

Just like those aliens.

Good thing that's just a bad piece of science fiction, isn't it?

#

"We need to think about this from his perspective," I say to Ouyang.

"His?" It takes a full three seconds for my advisor to figure out what I mean. "Who? The primitive?"

"His name is Balin. We should make him the focus, and construct an environment that will put him at ease, rather than cheap tourist scenes we imagine he'll enjoy."

"What are you talking about? You should be concerned about how you're going to finish your project and get your degree, instead of worrying about the feelings of some primitive. Don't waste my time."

Mr. Lu once said that the progress of a civilization should be measured by its degree of empathy – whether members of the civilization are capable of thinking from the values and perspectives of others – and not some other objectified scale.

Silently, I stare at Ouyang's face, trying to discern some trace of civilization.

The face, so carefully maintained to be wrinkle-free, is a wasteland.

I decide to work on the problem myself. Several younger students join me on their own initiative, restoring some of my faith in humanity. To be sure, most of them are motivated by their hatred of Ouyang, and it's not a bad way to earn a few credits.

There's a virtual reality program called iDealism, which claims to be capable of generating an environment based on brainwave patterns. In reality, all it does is selecting pre-existing models from a database whose brainwave signatures match the user's – at most it adds some high-resolution transitions. We hacked it for our own use, and since our lab's sensors are several orders of magnitude more sensitive than consumer-grade sensors, we add a lot of new measurement axes to the software and connect it to the largest open-source database, which contains demo data from virtual reality labs from around the world.

And now, Balin is going to be the Prime Mover of this virtual universe.

He will have plenty of time to explore the linkage between this world and every thought in his mind. I will record every move and gesture Balin makes. Then, when he returns to the real world, I will reconnect with him. I will imitate to the best of my ability each of his gestures. The two of us will be as two parallel mirrors, reflecting each other endlessly.

I put the helmet on Balin's head. His gaze is as placid as water.

The red light flashes, speeds up, turns green.

I enter Ghost mode, and bring up a third-person POV window in the upper-right hand corner. In it, I see a tiny avatar of Balin trembling in place.

Balin's world is primordial chaos. There is no earth, no heaven, no east, west, north or south. I struggle against the vertigo.

Finally, he stops shaking. A flash of lightning slowly divides the chaos, determining the location of the sky.

The lightning extends, limning a massive eye in the cloud cover. A web of fine lightning feelers spreads from the eye in every direction.

The light fades. Balin lifts his head and raises his hands. Rain falls.

He begins to dance.

Drops of rain fall with laughter, giving substance to the outline of wind. The wind lifts Balin until he is floating in the air, twirling about.

It is impossible to describe his dance in words. It is as if he has become a part of all Creation, and the heavens and the earth both respond to his movements and change.

My heart speeds up; my throat is dry; my hands and feet are icy cold. I'm witnessing an unsought miracle.

He lifts his hand and flowers bloom. He lifts his foot and birds flutter forth.

Balin dances between unnamed peaks, above unmapped lakes. Everywhere he sets foot, joyful mandalas bloom and spread, and he falls into their swirling, colorful centers.

One moment he is smaller than an atom, the next he encompasses the universe. All scales have lost meaning in his dance.

Every nameless life sings to him. He opens his mouth, and all the gods of the *paoxiao* emerge from his lips.

The spirits meld into his black skin like dark waves that rage and erupt, sweeping him up, up into the air. Behind him, the waves coalesce into an endless web on which all the fruits of creation may be found, each playing its own rhythm. A hundred million billion species are in search of their common origin.

I understand now.

In Balin's eyes, the soul is immanent in all Creation, and there is no difference between a dragonfly and a man. His nervous system is constructed in such a way as to allow him to empathize with the universe. It is impossible to imagine how much effort he must put into calming the tsunamis that rage constantly in his heart.

Even someone as unenlightened as me cannot be unmoved when faced with this grand spectacle produced by all Life. My eyes swim in hot tears, and threads of ecstasy inside my heart are woven with the dizzying sights in my vision. I stand atop a peak, but a step away from transcendence.

As for the answer I was seeking? I don't think it's so important anymore.

Balin absorbs everything into his body. His avatar expands rapidly and then deflates.

He falls.

The world dims, grows indistinct, lifeless.

Balin is like a thin film stretched against the tumbling, twirling space-time. The physics engine's algorithms undulate the edge of his body as though blown by a wind, and fragments rise into the air like a flock of birds.

His shape is disintegrating, dissolving.

#

I disconnect Balin from the VR system and take off his helmet.

He lies facedown on the soft, dark gray floor, his limbs spread out, unmoving.

"Balin?" I don't dare move him.

"Balin?" Everyone in the lab is waiting. Will this joke of an experiment turn into a tragedy?

Slowly, he shifts in place. Then he wriggles to the side like a pond loach until he is once again flattened against the floor, adopting the posture of a gecko.

I laugh. Like my father years ago, I clap my hands twice.

Balin turns, sits up, stares at me.

It is just like that hot and sticky summer night the year I turned thirteen, when we first met.

*Translated by Ken Liu*

笛安

# Di An

Di An, the daughter of two well-known authors, Li Rui and Jiang Yun, began writing in 2002, and her first novella *Sister's Forest* appeared in *Harvest* magazine. Her first novel, *Farewell to Heaven*, followed in 2005. In 2009 she became a best-selling author when the novel *City of the Dragon I* sold over 700,000 copies, and earned her a Most Promising Newcomer award at the Chinese Literature Media awards. Her most recent novel, *Ling Yang in the South*, finds her departing from fantasy and exploring historical fiction. She currently edits the bimonthly magazine *ZUI Found*.

西出阳关

# Beyond the Western Pass

### By Di An

I know that my end of days is this day, is right now. I'm already old, in my last years of life. I talk less and less, because no one understands me when I do. I'm surrounded more and more frequently by random strangers. They ask: "Do you remember me? Do you recognize me?" Are you kidding? Why should I recognize them? So they straighten up and say with real or pretend sadness, "She doesn't recognize anyone." A calm male voice replies: "That's senility for you." I turn around in annoyance: "Who are you calling senile?" The calm voice remains calm, and continues: "She thinks she's nineteen again."

He's wrong. He's making it up. Just yesterday morning I remembered with total clarity things that happened when I was sixty. I can clearly recall one evening of that year: an endless highway at night, dotted with streetlights on both sides. Although sixty may already be long gone, I'm not just some Alzheimer's patient trying to believe she's nineteen – yes, let us use the disease's official name, not "senile." I know perfectly well that I'm very old. All the smooth-skinned young women in their pretty poses must think I'm a monster. The man with the calm, assured voice calls me "Mom," which is the most absurd thing I've ever heard. Just a minute ago, I said to him: "When I'm dead, please put that picture of me at twenty-four on the gravestone." (See? I remember more than just being nineteen.) He looked at me suspiciously. Then I remembered that when I was twenty-four, he didn't exist – if what he says is true, and I gave birth to him. So I explained: "That picture I took when I was young, in Amsterdam. I was wearing a white blouse and standing next to the tulips." That is my absolute favorite picture, because it was taken when I was in my prime, and at my prettiest. To me, Amsterdam is frozen in a moment that is already a half century gone. Like the northern industrial city where I was born and raised, it exists now only as a clutter of disconnected episodes of memory. For instance: I can't remember what tulips look like, but I'll never forget the houseboats that floated in those narrow dikes. People lived in them. Only when memory turns fragmented and illogical does it become truly reliable, an integral part of a person's spirit. This is something a person cannot possibly realize while they are young.

Yet the tranquil stranger in front of me smiled and said: "Mom," – God, that word makes me angry – "that's impossible. No one puts a picture of when they were young on their grave." Forget it, forget it. People on the brink of death like me have one advantage: we no longer hold our hopes out for anything.

I've fallen asleep again; I'm dreaming, again. As I lose consciousness I hear the tranquil stranger say to a guest: "I'm really sorry, could you come again tomorrow, thank you for the flowers, she sleeps over ten hours a day now, just like a baby – if you come before lunch tomorrow, you might catch her awake, though of course, even if she is awake she may not recognize you."

Every time I fall asleep, the blue horse enters my dream and summons me to go. I follow it, and we run together; for this old body of mine to feel that light, floating step is exhilarating almost to the point of terror. I have always reacted to ecstasy with fear, since I was a child, like I were getting something I didn't deserve. But no one is interested in my childhood any more. People frequently lack imagination, and are unwilling to conceive of an old person having had a childhood. The blue horse is beautiful: it is the grey-blue color of the earth and sky in the minutes just before sunrise. There are subtle streaks of red in its mane and tail, as if it were cut whole-cloth out of the dawn.

In this dream I am always nineteen. Why, I don't know. But I don't scrutinize anything closely anymore. The blue horse is so kind to me, and when it looks at me with those huge, limpid eyes, I remember what it feels like to be a young woman. "Young woman" isn't a noun or a rhetorical device, let alone an excuse for narcissism – it is the undeniably genuine feeling that one could be carried away by the energy of one's spirit at any moment. I'm nineteen, and I'm wearing the clothes I wore that year: a bright red dress. The color and cut are absolutely horrible, but that isn't important, because youth is always disarrayed. When you're no longer in disarray, your cleanest days are past. The blue horse smiles – don't ask me how a horse could smile, I just know it was smiling – and says: "Do you like the way you look now, my dear?" It looks at me, eyes as soft as water and sad as ice. The breath from its nostrils tickles my ear and cheek. As it gives a coquettish toss of its mane I am struck with the truth: I finally understand why I am always nineteen when I am here, and who the horse is.

Nineteen was the year I started writing stories. You could say that was the year my life truly began; you could also say that was the year I said goodbye to a real life. This horse, this blue horse, represents my stories.

When I was young, the books I wrote were read by other young people. Now they are all old, and so am I. I have no strength left for writing, nor they for reading. Thus history surreptitiously ends one cycle and begins another.

The blue horse steals on in its noiseless gallop. A nineteen-year-old me in a horrid red dress sits on his back. We flee through the dream of the dying. "You know you're going to die?" it asks. I reply: "Will you die with me?" It laughs drily. "Good God, you haven't changed at all. Still as selfish and overbearing as ever."

Even in my nineteen-year-old body I can feel that I am near the end. I am losing the power of thought, and of language, which is to say that I'm losing all capability to interact with the world. So my final hour is arriving, and the blue horse comes to find me.

I can no longer remember any detail of my relationship with my stories. I only know that we were inseparable for a long time – you could even say we kept each other alive. The blue horse's body heat effaces all memory of hardship. He carries me over great distances – yes, I can still remember, my stories and I traveled a long, hard road together. And I remember that road got more and more desolate.

Illustration by Wang Yan

"Is there an end or not?" I ask the blue horse.

He chuckles softly. "How should I know? I was going to ask you."

"If I told you that I didn't know if there were an end, would you still be willing to go with me?" Was that really my voice? My voice at nineteen really was clear, and full of that uncertainty peculiar to the young.

"Are you kidding?" It turns to look at me. "Obviously, you're the one who's sticking to me no matter what. I can't get rid of you. What a headache." It bats its eyelashes at me. I am suddenly caught in a storm of recollection.

I leave all my hopes to the sound of earthly applause; I leave all my tears to the men I once loved; I leave all my worries to my departed parents and the son I no longer recognize, and I leave all my happiness and disappointment to this beaten, scarred, and leaky thing called life. I have absolutely nothing to say to the world. All elegant affectations are exercises in futility, all great beliefs and profound emotions are mirages and delusion. I want nothing but to continue this tireless sprint with the blue horse, because in life I gave what came from the deepest recesses of my soul to my writing – it wasn't hope, nor sorrow, nor worry nor joy nor disappointment nor any kind of love or hate. Humanity hasn't devised a word for it yet, which is why it can remain so distinct and soft, without any trace of having been invaded by language.

Over this road that is my life, the blue horse and I pass by an abandoned railway station, an old smelting factory, and countless gravestones in the rain. The petals of fresh flowers fall as they wish onto the names of the dead. Then there is emptiness, without even graveyards. The flat, red earth cracks. At the horizon, a peach blossom opens in a howl of color, yet it is forever unapproachable. I do not ask the blue horse where we are, it merely asks me: "Are you sure you want to keep going?" I respond: "I'm sure." Of course, I'm terrified, fear sweeps through me like a wind, but when one has no sense of direction, what is there to do but advance? To turn around and go back is what takes real courage.

"Our water is almost gone." I say to the blue horse.

It smiles kindly, and says: "I'm fine. I can live without eating or drinking. Save it all for yourself."

The sky darkens. Evening on the plain is cold. The blue horse lies gracefully on one side, and I snuggle against it, my arms wrapped tightly around its belly for warmth. This is when I notice the priest. He sits on the bare earth not far from me, his black cassock covered with dust, his lips so dry and cracked they bleed, yet with a look of peace in his eyes.

He watches me for a long interval.

"Come with me," he says. "I can see you yearn for the religious life."

I say: "No."

"Why not?" asks the priest. "I'll take you to Heaven. I know the way."

I hesitate. The blue horse tilts its head to look at me. "I certainly don't know the way. Go with whomever you'd like."

I give all the water I have with me to the priest. I am sincere. I say to him: "Please forgive me. I don't think I'll be going to Heaven. At least, not right now."

He brushes the dust from his robe, smiles, and leaves us. "You sure are stubborn," sighs the blue horse.

"Will I die of thirst?" I ask the horse. It replies: "If you die, I'll just keep going. I'll run into someone else like you eventually, and take them with me; then, when they die, I'll go on alone again. It's incredibly liberating."

I smile. "How heartbreaking." It replies: "Not exactly. If you were to live forever, I would have to die; only by your death am I able to stay alive."

"So we're enemies?" I ask. It considers the question, then says: "Not exactly. Even though I exchange your death for my own survival, I also warm your memory of living."

It reared and gave a long, alluring whinny that startled a few crows by the horizon. "Come on, get on my back. I'll make a bet with you: I'll carry you straight in a random direction, and see if I can't bring you out." I lie down on its back, and it resumes his noiseless gallop. Its hooves kick up thick grains of sand that sting my face. I close my eyes, and whisper in its ear: "Maybe we'll even find a river, and some evidence of life." It laughs at me gently. "What signs of life? This barren plain we're on right now is your own dying mind. The only sign of life is this adolescent image of you in a red dress. Do you still not understand?"

At some point, I'm not sure when, it pulls up. The stop is so sudden it almost jolts me off his back. We stand in front of a battlefield fresh with slaughter. Blood runs in rivers; the sun slips in by accident and is stained red. The eye can see nothing but mangled corpses. What were once strong, nimble arms hang from the dead branch of a tree. My blue horse accidentally steps in a dying charger's eye socket. I shiver, and say: "Let's go. You've brought me to the only place that could be worse than a wasteland."

"Have I?" The blue horse smiles as it stares at the head of a general, beached on the sand banks of the blood river. "Do you not recognize it? This bloodied battlefield is really just your attachment to the world."

Night falls. I am dizzy with thirst. I had thought that this young dream-body would be resilient, since it is no more than a spirit. Sadly, I was wrong. I am still fragile. "What a pity," I smile weakly, "I can't go with you any farther. But I want to ask you: if you've known so many like me already, have you ever taken anyone all the way out? Can you tell me what's at the end of the wasteland?"

The horse lowers its proud, beautiful head, and tenderly licks my face. Just as my hearing evaporates into mist, I think I hear it say, "If you want to get out…" Then I hear no more. My red dress melts away.

Then I wake up. Everything around me feels strange. The tranquil stranger walks over and says: "Mom, you're awake." I still don't recognize him. But I suddenly know what it is I have to do.

The tranquil stranger takes me for a stroll in the park. It isn't really a "stroll," of course – I just sit in the wheelchair and sunbathe. He bends down to button my sweater for me. With a smile he says: "Mom, you're just as pretty as you were at nineteen." He's lying. But I like to hear it anyway. I stare without blinking at a cold drinks vendor in front of us: rainbow-dazzling mounds of shaved ice shine in the clown's hand like the shouts of children. "Mom, do you want some shaved ice?" He laughs and shakes his head. "Ma, you really have turned back into a child. All right, wait just a second." His silhouette gets smaller as he walks away and then stops in front of the clown. I propel my wheelchair as fast as I can into a stand of trees. Here the land falls away in an apocalyptic slope of vertiginous steepness.

A child is standing in front of my wheelchair, looking at me with a clear curiosity. "Be a good boy and do something for me," I say. "Help me out and that nice man will give you shaved ice." He nods and says, "OK."

I say: "Push me as fast as you can, and when we get to this hill, let go. It's simple. You'll do this for me, won't you?" He is quiet for a moment, then his face twists in a crafty smile and I catch a familiar flash of blue in his eyes. "You're here," I say.

"I'm here." His voice is so soft, his tone of voice so old.

"Let's go, then."

The scenery around me begins to blur. The wind at my ears is wonderfully crisp and cool. I close my eyes to enjoy this incredible speed, ignoring the alarmed cries of people around me. As the pace quickens, I feel like I'm a child again, going down a slide: time flows backwards.

The first time I sensed my death was near was at the funeral of my best friend; torrential rain on the day my child's child was born, and the strange, grey lights in the hospital; the doctor saying to me, "Congratulations, you're pregnant!" and hearing a strange buzzing in my ear, like an insect about to be entombed in amber; the tranquil stranger's father and I building a fire beneath a pale *aurora borealis* at New Year, the sparks that hovered in the endless waste representing all of life's illusions; the smell of fresh grass in the summer of my seventeenth year; losing a red balloon when I was small, and my mother saying, "Don't cry, honey, Mommy will buy you a new one…" Then comes a loud bang, then darkness; then I begin to fly, I transform into a beam of light. In this moment, I realize what it was the blue horse had said to me at the end of my dream: "If you want to get out, you have to learn not to hold on to the illusion of 'I'." But there is no time for me to put this into a novel; I am no longer I; I am a beam of light.

This is what I want to leave to the world. My horse, my stories and I have already drunk our last cup of wine. Death is no great event. I have gone beyond the Western pass, and have no need for familiar faces.

*Translated by Canaan Morse*

宫梓铭

# Gong Ziming

Gong Ziming was born in 2002. He is a student at the International section of Beijing National Day School. His stories *Poets: God and the Programmer*, *Jealousy*, his essay collection *Changbai Mountain*, and more were published in newspapers and magazines.

# 似曾相识

# Déjà vu

## By Gong Ziming

I t all began with a dream and a book that went missing.

The owner of this book was Mr Gu, who lived in a small town in southern China. The town was situated on a riverbank, alongside which grew many willow trees. In the winter these willow trees were obscured by the thick fog, and in August they swayed under the sun's rays, their leaves refracting the sunlight, which passed through the early morning breeze, illuminating the air's fluttering particles. Willow trees also grew on both sides of the small town's two perpendicular main roads, and it was at the library situated at the junction of these roads that Mr Gu worked. This librarian's workload was sometimes light and sometimes heavy – depending on the secondary school next door. Just before the start of a new term, the students swarmed into the tiny library, scrambling to get their hands on its small supply of books. The library also sold stationery, which meant it saw a fair flow of customers on weekdays. During the winter and summer holidays, the narrow space between the grey walls became much more capacious. At these times,

Mr Gu would bring along his own book, pull up a chair and sit down to read.

One August weekend afternoon dominated by willow trees and sunshine, his colleagues all trickled off somewhere. The library was extremely quiet, and it was almost as if you could hear the sound of the walls cracking from the potent rays of the sun. He sat down to read Borges' *The Garden of Forking Paths*, which he'd brought to work with him. As Mr Gu was reading, he heard the door being pushed open, so he got up and walked towards the entrance, where he found a secondary school student dressed in a thick winter uniform searching the shelves. It wasn't the uniform of the school next door. Aren't you hot? Mr Gu asked the student, who hesitated before responding that he was fine. What book do you want to borrow? Mr Gu asked, and the student said I don't know, I'm just browsing. With nothing better to do, the small town librarian wandered along with him, a bookshelf between them.

Suddenly piqued by curiosity, Mr Gu asked why he'd come to the library. Because I have this strong recollection of borrowing a book from this library, the student said. It was a great story, very intriguing, but then I forgot to return it. It was a very thin book with a yellow cover, the student added, but I've forgotten the title.

Maybe I can help by checking the borrowing records, Mr. Gu said. From your accent I'm assuming you're not from around here. I only arrived here yesterday, and it's my first time visiting, the student said. Mr Gu felt a bit baffled by this. How did you manage to borrow the book then? The student fell silent, and it was a long time before he spoke again: "In actual fact, I also have a clear recollection of meeting you."

Mr Gu smiled and said, "Why can't I remember you then? There aren't many new faces around here." He continued to walk along.

"I also remember what you're going to say next."

"Go on then."

"You're going to say: in that case you must be a prophet. And I reply: Who knows – perhaps these memories are a dream. Then you say: do you always have the feeling that everything has happened before? And I say, yes. Then I say, you'll understand. You say, That's very strange. "

The librarian was dumbstruck, because that really was what he'd been about to say. While this was happening, the student's footsteps stopped suddenly, and he pulled a book from the shelf with a laugh: Ah, here it is. He ran to the entrance, where he wrote the title and his own name down in the borrowing record, thanked Mr Gu and left. Being in such a rush, the student didn't close the library door properly after himself. A gust of wind blew through, and the heavy glass door slammed against its frame.

Mr Gu suddenly came to, glancing at the faint silhouette through the closed door. He raced to the door, but the figure had disappeared. He returned to check the record book, but could find no entry for anyone borrowing a book that day. For the next hour, Mr Gu inspected all the bookshelves he remembered walking along with the student, but couldn't see that anything was missing. However, returning to his chair he discovered his copy of *The Garden of Forking Paths* gone.

He spent the next half hour anxiously looking around for it, without any joy. He walked wearily outside for some fresh air. It was three p.m., the slow and easy afternoon was just winding down and the little town coming back to life. He looked up at the blue sky, not one bird in it. Between the willow trees that ran along both sides of the street there was nothing but open sky and floating clouds. He was hit with a strong sense of familiarity, as if he'd lived through all this before. The catkin-shaped clouds right in the middle of the sky would float northwards, the proprietress of the fruit shop would tip a bucket of grimy water onto the street, a red Santana would drive slowly out from the crossing. Cumulatively, these images built up a sense of déjà vu, which made him feel panicky. Mr Gu looked to the opposite side of the street where he saw a security guard dozing in front of the shopping centre. "Not long from now, a car is going to drive past the shopping centre, and the security guard will wake up with a jolt," he thought with glee. He waited for what felt like an age, while the security guard continued to doze peacefully. Mr Gu gave a quiet chuckle, and turned around, noticing his reflection in the glass door looking drawn and bored beyond belief. He rubbed his eyes, thinking, it's just another boring afternoon, and I had a boring dream. I've just experienced some weird hallucinations, that's all. Just then, a car engine behind him let off a terrifying noise. He turned his head to see the shopping centre security guard being jolted awake.

Mr Gu spent many days engaged in similar activities, making use of these prophet-like qualities. At first he had clear visions of everything that would happen some thirty seconds into the future. He was delighted with his "skill" and popped up childishly all over town, curiously exploring all its corners, and finding out if reality would confirm the ideas that sparked in his mind. He played this game again and again, successfully each time. While chatting with colleagues, he loved suddenly blurting out what the other person was about to say, getting a kick out of the incredulous, surprised or delighted looks on their faces.

This honeymoon period didn't last very long.

Soon, everything became dull. His perception wasn't as keen as it had been, and he no longer knew ahead of time how things were going to unfold. His ability for prophecy faded into a sense of déjà vu. To be specific, it was like having a malicious little fellow by his ear spoiling the plot of everything that was about to happen. He experienced all events as if they had already happened thousands of times before. It's all already happened, he thought in despair, but it's only the split second before it happens that I become aware of it. Life slowly became unbearable. It was like a living hallucination, or sinking through the quicksand of memory, unable to lift himself free.

He lived in this tragic way for four months, his symptoms getting progressively worse. At the beginning, it was still relatively simple things, then it was TV dramas, films and books, after that it was internet chat forums, and the next casualty was music.

By autumn, he had lost interest in looking at satellite maps, which was odd – the orderly arrangements of land within satellite maps had always given him a huge spiritual boost. One day in early winter, he returned home and picked up a book, only to have the shocking realisation that his symptoms had become so severe that they were affecting his reading. After that all books became dreary – the final barricade of the fortress of reality crumbled. He decided to go to the hospital.

There was a metal shop next to the hospital where construction was being carried out, and Mr Gu's eyes were captivated by the flying dust.

He walked inside to the reception hall, where he was greeted by a huge din. Crowds of people stood before the registration desk, throngs of panicky parents holding their children and charging against the crowd, and throngs of emaciated patients standing propped up against the wall. Mr Gu suddenly felt at peace, and it was only after some time that he understood: this chaotic and noisy scene had overwhelmed his ability to tell the future. Right in the middle of his field of vision he still had that sense of familiarity, but from the corners of his eyes, that delightful sense of the unknown had returned. He stood in the middle of the hall, breathing deeply, savouring that sweet moment.

Just then he spotted Dr Wang, his good friend. When his symptoms first appeared, Dr. Wang had advised Mr Gu to seek medical attention. Unfortunately there was nowhere you could go to cure an illness like this. And so today, Dr Wang had asked his former schoolmate, a consultant psychologist, to pay a visit. He had been a very capable student, Dr Wang had explained to Mr Gu, and so Mr Gu had come to the hospital especially. Dr Wang walked over and said, "How have you been?"

"I can't read any longer. It's causing me real grief."

"Didn't I tell you to go seek immediate medical attention? The consultant is in my office."

"Aren't you on duty?"

"I am. But it's not too busy. There are only a few patients in Ophthalmology. Unlike Paediatrics, which is rammed." Dr Wang put both hands in his pockets, and sized Mr Gu up for a moment. "Still working in the library then?"

"Yep."

Illustration by Wang Yan

"Waste of talent," the doctor said, without a hint of ridicule. "I must get back to work. Make your way upstairs and find him."

Mr Gu walked up the stairs in a daze, and along to Mr Wang's office. He opened the door to find a young man in a checked shirt sitting inside. The young man stood up. "Mr Gu, is it?"

"Yes. And how should I address you?"

"Please call me Zhao." Seeing Mr Gu's slightly puzzled expression he said, "Have you not experienced this before?"

"No, I haven't. I only began getting symptoms this summer."

"Ah, sorry, I meant seeing a psychologist."

"Oh, no, never."

"That's normal. I'll just put this out there before we start: I'm working for an internet company at the moment, as a programmer."

"Ah…"

"I was indeed Dr Wang's schoolmate in the psychology department at medical college. But later, I changed degrees – which makes me a dabbler, I suppose. I'm not going to lie to you, this is the first time I've ever carried out a patient consultation."

"I understand. In a small town like this, there's a lack of fully-trained professionals."

The young man gave an uncomfortable laugh.

"Of course, that's not to say you…." Mr Gu hurried to correct himself.

"It's fine. Let's get down to it. My understanding is that since August you've been having symptoms of cryptomnesia."

"Cryptomnesia?" Mr Gu had a vague sense that he'd heard this word before.

"The sense that something feels very familiar."

"Yes, exactly. Since August."

"Can you describe your symptoms in detail?"

Mr Gu spent the next twenty minutes moaning to the young man about all the perplexing things he'd had to endure, and gave a detailed description of how his symptoms had gotten worse: from something near "prophecy" to that constant feeling of "déjà vu"; from real life events at the beginning, to later when it had affected TV programmes, music and books.

The young man listened to his lament, then said, "Your symptoms are much more severe than I imagined. I'm not going to lie, I have no idea what's causing this. But, generally, such a feeling is known as fausse reconnaissance. It's when you think you've experienced something before. One theory has it that fausse reconnaissance is caused by a small disturbance occurring in the part of the brain entrusted with dates and time. When you start to experience an event, your brain stores it, but it doesn't remember the time the event actually occurred. Therefore, as the thing continues to happen, you feel as if it has happened before. That's it in a nutshell."

"Why would I develop such a condition?"

"Many people are susceptible to fausse reconnaissance, but it's the first time I've come across a case where it is continuous and sustained over such a long period. I haven't seen many people with fausse reconnaissance… but, generally, the intensification of déjà vu is brought about by damage to the prefrontal lobe. Did you hit your head at some point around the time of the onset of the symptoms?"

Mr Gu thought a moment. "No, I didn't," he said. "I had a dream, actually. About someone who had a strong sense of déjà vu."

The young man fell silent for a while before saying, "I'm sorry, I have no cure for you."

"Thanks anyway."

"Having said that, how long have you lived in this town?"

"Apart from the four years I was at university, I've lived here all my life. Twenty-eight years in total."

"Right then. What I'm going to say now is pure guesswork – fantastical thinking, if you like. But what if your unconscious mind is completely bored and fed up of living in this town? It's such a small place, and it's barely changed at all in the past few decades. Your brain will naturally have become all too familiar with the details, which means you can more or less work out all the trends of what is about to happen. This minor distortion to your memory is therefore causing you to generate this sense of déjà vu. While this theory doesn't explain the phenomenon you are experiencing when it comes to music and books, it offers a partial explanation of the issue. In my opinion, you should book some time off work and visit somewhere you've never been before, get to experience what it's like to feel 'the unfamiliar'."

"Ah, good idea. Thank you."

"You're very welcome. If there's nothing else, I'll be off now." The young man stood up and left. Mr Gu remained sitting in a daze for some time, staring out the window at the fog outside.

For the Spring Festival break, Mr Gu bought himself a train ticket to visit a big city, leaving on the evening of New Year's Eve. Before setting off, he sat on his own in the library, hands curled up inside his sleeves. The little town had become very animated, but as usual, the library was its forgotten corner. Just as he was feeling so bored he was about to nod off, he heard the door being pushed open. So Mr Gu got up and walked towards the entrance, where he found a secondary school student dressed in a thick winter uniform searching the shelves. It wasn't the uniform of the school next door.

"What book do you want to borrow?"

"I don't know, I'm just browsing."

Mr Gu stared at him a while before asking, "Are you looking for Borges' *The Garden of Forking Paths*?"

"Yeah, I think that's the one. I have this strong recollection of borrowing a book from this library. It was a great story, very intriguing, but then I forgot to return it. It was a very thin book with a yellow cover, it might be the one you just mentioned."

Mr Gu knew that he should say: "From your accent I'm assuming you're not from around here." But led by some strange force, he heard himself instead saying, "I've seen you before. You told me you always have this feeling that everything has happened before."

The student raised his head in shock. "But I don't think I've ever seen you before? I do have that feeling though."

"I have the same condition as you, I understand it now."

"Understand what?"

"It doesn't matter. Forget I said anything. Always having a sense of déjà vu is certainly very annoying."

"Tell me about it – it's very hard to deal with. I'm slowly getting used to it though."

The student looked for a long time, and then shook his head in disappointment.

"Can't find it?"

"No."

"That's very strange indeed."

"Why?"

"Because I remember you finding it."

The student wrinkled his brow in suspicion. "You must be an actual prophet, in that case."

"Who knows."

When he'd seen the student out, Mr Gu picked up his case and headed to the station. He boarded the train, heading north. There were very few people in his carriage, and the only person who shared his row of seats was a fat balding guy taking a nap. The librarian looked out the window, his breath fogging up the glass. Outside, he saw night descending onto the vast North China Plain. There were no stars to be seen. The sky was a deep, deep blue, just like ink or the depths of the ocean. The odd cloud that did appear would be gloomifed by the dark sky. In the distance, the last trace of dusk could be seen, a glow along the horizon. Putting his face closer to the glass, villages came into view, one after the other, trees at their entrances, leafless all of them; every so often a dog let out a whimper. These scenes were all new to him, yet they felt very familiar. He stared out of the window, until that last dot of orangey-yellow in the distance was gone. When he awoke, they'd pulled up at the station. He stepped down onto the platform. He stood in front of the frisbee-shaped station staring blankly at the road. A while later, he was waiting to hail a taxi. No drivers were still out working at that hour. By the time a taxi arrived, Mr Gu's hands were nearly frozen. He got in the car, the warm air fogging up his glasses. Where are you going? asked the driver. Which is the tallest building in the city? Mr Gu asked. The driver pointed to the right past the windshield and told him, Look, that's the one. Let's go there then, Mr Gu said. The driver put the meter on, and set off in the direction of the tall building. En route Mr. Gu fell asleep again, dreaming that he was back at university, where his professor smiled as he told him: Your work is going to be published, it's going to be in the evening paper. He smiled back as he replied: In that case I must thank you, my teacher, for nurturing me. The newspaper editor has come to discuss the publication with you face to face, the professor told him. Here, this is Editor Li. The person who'd just been introduced as Editor Li walked over from the side, and it was the student he'd seen in his small town. The student said, "I always have the feeling that everything's happened before. Do you know what I mean?"

"We're here," the driver yelled. Mr Gu opened his eyes and saw a towering building before him. He walked towards the main entrance, but found the door locked. He walked all the way round the building, discovering a small unlocked door, which he pushed open and walked through. There was a lift behind the door, but no light. He stood in the darkness waiting for the lift. The lift had a light on inside it, as if it had been waiting for this uninvited guest. He got into the lift and pressed the button for the top floor.

The lift door opened. The corridor in front of him was completely dark. He walked along it, and the lift door closed behind him, taking away the last bit of light. He saw there was a window straight ahead, outside of which he could see the starry sky.

How strange, thought Mr Gu, how could I be seeing stars here. On his left was a door, locked. Turning to his right, he found another door, this one unlatched. Walking through it, Mr Gu discovered a group of people sitting down. He found himself walking into the room, locating a free seat and sitting down. The people were discussing something or other. From listening to the elderly man in charge, he understood that they had just finished talking about time and eternity, and were moving on to a discussion about fear.

One woman explained in a gentle voice how she was a student from the history department, and always turned into historical figures in her dreams. One time, she'd been researching the riot between the eight princes of the western Jin dynasty, and just before going to bed she'd read about the Changsha king Sima Yi's death. In the dream, she turned into Sima Yi. It was the twenty-seventh day of the first month of the lunar year, and the king was burned to death by the enemy in the city of Jinyu. Since then she had been completely terrified of fire. One man said he constantly saw tall thin people wearing top hats. All they did was smile. Nothing but smile. These people terrified him. A far-away voice talked about being scared of the void, about being afraid that nothing really existed. Someone else said that the thing that scared him most was cats' eyes. Then it was Mr. Gu's turn.

"I've always been scared of loops," he said, "and the minute changes that occur within loops. When I was very young I had a dream, it may have been a dream, it may have been real, who knows what a small child sees – I was at home, sitting on the floor, watching two people on the television who were both sitting watching television themselves. On the television within the television there were also two people and a television. My field of vision started to move, crossing through endless televisions nestled inside each other, into infinity. This never-ending loop was scary enough as it was. But, when my field of vision reached a certain depth, the two people started to turn their heads. Because each moment my vision would enter into the next television in the sequence, their heads would return to the original position; but each time their heads turned a little further, a little further still. I had no idea when it would reach the end. In theory, I should have been afraid of these two strange people's faces, but later, I started to feel excited, it felt like I was praying for freedom.

"A few months ago, I developed a strange illness. I started to feel like everything before me had already happened. A psychologist consultant told me this was called fausse reconnaissance. I don't know if it is or not. He told me I should go in search of the unfamiliar. And that's why I'm here. I thought, if I'd had these symptoms during the television dream, would that have made the experience more comfortable? I've lived in a small town for twenty-eight years, working as a librarian, which is nothing like how I envisaged I'd spend my life. Nothing ever changes there. Every day is the same as water. Every day is like a loop, and what is worse, there's not even a segment where the heads turn. I'm thinking that maybe this condition has come about in order to cure me of my fear. Perhaps. Oh, I have met someone else with this illness, but I don't know if he's also scared of loops. I'm sorry, I've gone on too long, it's just I'm so confused. It wasn't my intention to disrupt you all, I came in because of my condition; this room felt very familiar. In actual fact, I don't know any of you. I apologise, as soon as I started talking I couldn't stop. You carry on. As you were, please."

After Mr Gu stopped talking, there was silence which continued for a long time. The elderly man broke it: "You spoke very well. It's a good story. Out of gratitude, I would like to offer you a book, if I may? It could help to enlighten you."

Mr Gu looked at him dubiously.

The elderly man pulled out a yellow book, very thin. "This is Borges' *The Garden of Forking Paths*. It's for you."

Mr Gu took the book from him, lifted his head, and saw the starry sky outside; it all felt very unknown.

*Translated by Poppy Toland*

潘向黎

# Pan Xiangli

Pan Xiangli was born in 1966 in Quanzhou, Fujian province, and later moved to Shanghai. From 1991 to 1998, she worked as an editor for *Shanghai Literature* and also attended Tokyo University of Foreign Studies from 1992 to 1994. She began publishing her writing in 1988: her story collections include *Following Along Without a Dream*, *The Decade Cup*, *A Soft Touch*, *I Love Maruko Chan*; and her essay collections include *Red Dust*, *White Feathers*, *The Age of Innocence*, *The Age of Believing in Love*, and *Sometimes the Parts Are Perfect*. Her short story *Western Wind, Long Street* received *Shanghai Literature*'s prize for outstanding work, and she has also received a literary award from the *Wenhui Daily* Pen Association. Her short story *Vegetable Soup* won the 4th Lu Xun Literature Prize.

雪深一尺，我在美浓等你

# Snow Deep, I'll Be Waiting for You at Mei Nong

By Pan Xiangli

I t's raining, the last rain of the fall or the first one of the winter. You don't have to worry, I'm not getting wet out there in the rain, I'm sitting here at Mei Nong Café, warm and dry.

Coffee is brewing, exuding its life's strongest aroma. Mr. Hu starts to grind beans and make coffee once he sees me come in. I've been coming to this place so often that verbal greetings are no longer necessary. Sometimes I think that if I were in trouble some day and barely had money for food, I could still count on Mei Nong, even in a metropolis the size of Shanghai. That's the benefit of being a regular customer.

I've heard that Beethoven counted out 60 coffee beans every morning to be ground and brewed. Does Mr. Hu count his beans every time he makes coffee? Maybe he just estimates the amount, which should be precise enough for someone of his experience. But when I sit in the loft of Mei Nong, I always tend to imagine that he's downstairs counting coffee beans, not using a metal scoop to heap out the beans like a sales-clerk in some food store.

The aroma of coffee rises, faintly first, then gathering into dense and tactile clouds that wrap around you, tight like reunited lovers hugging each other without a word. Such a strong aroma sometimes reminds me of the idiom: "no turning back." The scent of coffee is irresistible and intimate, yet when we humans devote ourselves to others with the same kind of commitment, this attentiveness often leads to alienation. Is this why, when I'm breathing in the coffee aroma, I'm at peace, neither wild with joy nor overly sad?

I take out a blue velvet bag from my purse, pull out a thin book – *The Little Prince* – and start reading it. It's always like this: if I have more than 45 minutes to spare at any particular place, I'll take *The Little Prince* out, find where I was last, and continue reading.

I could almost recite each line, but I still mark the page with a pale blue post-it before I close the book so I can find it easily next time. I read, again and again, continuously cycling through its pages.

I'm in luck today, no pale blue post-it to be found in the book, which means I've reached the end. So I turn to the beginning, no, to the dedication.

To Leon Werth

I ask children to forgive me for dedicating this book to a grown-up. I have a serious excuse: this grown-up is the best friend I have in the world. I have another excuse: this grown-up can understand everything, even books for children. I have a third excuse: he lives in France where he is hungry and cold. He needs to be comforted. If all these excuses are not enough, then I want to dedicate this book to the child whom this grown-up once was. All grown-ups were children first. (But few of them remember it.) So I correct my dedication:

To Leon Werth

When He Was a Little Boy

This is the most moving dedication I've ever read; straightforward and memorable – innocent yet full of sadness! A great writer can distinguish himself the moment he pens his first word.

Sometimes I'll think that you may have changed into a different person by now. I might be remembering and waiting for the old you. Even so, nothing can be changed. As the fox would say, I have been "tamed" by you.

I'll be waiting for you. If you have changed, I'll still be waiting for the person who you once were.

Mr. Hu knows that I don't need chitchat so he doesn't say anything when he brings me the coffee. He still brews me Mei Nong brand, using a 240cc large cup, and still only charges me for every other cup. The way he holds the coffee cup is still British style – the cup's ear on the left, so a righty will have to turn it around to drink the coffee. The ear will be on the right for the Americans.

You taught me this. You know lots of interesting yet useless trivia. But what else can you talk about in a café? Stocks and real estate? True coffee lovers would rather spend their time daydreaming in the coffee aroma, wasting their intelligence, indifferent to fame and wealth. In that moment, their bodies are here, but their souls fly to distant asteroids through a secret passage, veiled in coffee steam.

Successful men also visit coffee houses, but they don't belong there; only the real coffee lovers do. They tame the coffee house and are tamed by it in turn, each indispensable to the other.

Then there are the coffee maniacs who come to the café only to drink coffee. They are impatient, frowning now and then while waiting for their order, missing entirely the aroma of coffee beans being ground, brewed, or immersed. The café's history, its environment and the decoration, have no bearing on their desire for coffee. They are addicted to excessive coffee drinking, just like patients who are obsessed with taking medications right on the dot. If they are true coffee-men, then coffee-men are like unhealthy butterfly orchids, precarious and worrisome.

Real coffee lovers linger at coffee shops not only because they love coffee, but also because they want to feel free. They want to think of nothing. All their mundane tasks, worries, and distracting thoughts are like old coats that they want to take off and leave outside. Or perhaps it's because, in a café, they can contemplate anything they want. Dreams never come so close to reality; it feels like they will come true in the instant you step outside the café. This feeling of imminent accomplishment is irresistible.

It's not important what kind of coffee to have; it's even fine not to drink any. You can be a real coffee lover just by truly enjoying the aroma of coffee.

Yesterday, Xiao Ou gave me his wedding invitation. I congratulated him, but I couldn't pretend I was beaming with happiness. My last good friend was getting married and I felt lonely. But perhaps it's only out of habit that I say I "felt" lonely. I am lonely, and I always have been; friends getting married and having babies merely peels off the outer layer of my loneliness, making it naked and immediate.

"What's my present?" Xiao Ou said jokingly when he left.

"A cup of coffee as a goodbye gift," I said. We went to Enjoy. Enjoy is the place I go to meet with friends, just as Mei Nong has become the place I go by myself, now you've left.

I asked for my regular – Butterfly Pea. Xiao Ou ordered his usual Blue Mountain.

"Why are we this stubborn?" he said suddenly, looking at the coffee.

I didn't say anything. Relationships can be a lot like choosing coffee: sometimes you have to be stubborn. I have nothing to say.

"I just can't accept that this is it. At least give me one definite rejection," he said, after finishing his coffee.

"What is this nonsense? You're getting married."

"I'd cancel the wedding for you," he said.

I couldn't believe he was having this fantasy before the wedding. Such a heartless person. I never thought a coffee-man could be so capricious.

He got his rejection at last. We parted knowing that we probably wouldn't see each other again.

I suppose there really is a world of difference among people, "as vast as the gulf between the living and the dead," as you once said.

Saint-Exupéry wrote at the beginning of chapter two: "So I lived all alone, without anyone I could really talk to…" How sad. True though, for the most part. It's hard to find someone to have a real conversation with.

But you and I are different. Whatever we say to each other is instantly understood.

If I hadn't been taking shelter from a rain shower, I probably would have never walked into an old café like Mei Nong. So I have rain to thank.

"Mei Nong": beautiful and rich. It was a small place with simple decorations and five or six tables covered with red-white checkered tablecloth. The owner was about fifty, tall, with a straight back and a crew cut. He wore a long sleeve T-shirt, and was sharp and energetic.

I would come to learn that both he and his café embodied the kind of tranquility that belongs to the past.

I couldn't drink coffee then so I ordered a cocoa just to be polite. It was excellent, rich and steaming hot, with just the right amount of rum.

I savored my cocoa and was so surprised when I saw you come quietly downstairs. You were like a dazzling ray of afternoon sunlight, brightening up the entire café. Just like that, my impression of this place changed. I didn't even know there was another floor above this one. Or that this café would have a customer like you.

Illustration by Wang Yan

Such a fine, delicate face, or maybe "handsome" is a better term. In a crowded city where people avoid eye contact, you could make people do a double take. Nearly 5'9" tall, you were athletically built, yet your skin was the color of white ivory. Above your broad shoulders was a head of nicely trimmed hair, a lustrous, natural look. You wore a dark green turtle neck that drew out your neckline beautifully. Maybe I should not use such a term to describe a man, but the word "elegance" did cross my mind.

It's not like I haven't seen men who dress up decently and take good care of their looks, but I knew right away that you were something different. They are like pebbles, smooth from being scrubbed and soaked for a long time, or covered in moss, lovely and fresh. But you are a piece of jade.

I didn't see you pay. You said goodbye to Mr. Hu and looked past me, walked out into the rain without hesitation. You didn't have any rain gear, not even a jacket, but that didn't seem to bother you. You moved slowly, in a daze, as if you were just waking up from a dream, yet at the same time somehow decisive and alert.

I was curious about what might be upstairs, but too shy to go up.

The second time I came to Mei Nong was to see what the second floor was like. I climbed up the narrow wooden stairs without too much difficulty. It was really just a loft with a dormer window and a few tables. Same red-white checkered tablecloth.

The afternoon sun poured lazily into the loft, bringing a faint breath of fall leaves. It made me want to stretch out. I chose the table nearest the dormer window and sat where the light shone through from the left. I thought of the times I played house in the attics of my grandmother and my classmates' homes, the secrets I shared with my best friends, as well as my poor and simple college life.

I later learned that you and I picked the same table and I had sat where you usually sit. Back against the wall and facing the stairway. The seat is comfortable and safe, inviting you to spend eternity sitting there.

The day we met, you had the French edition of *The Little Prince* in your hand. You said it was a must read.

I didn't know French, and I didn't think there was an edition in

Chinese. So you read to me in our mother tongue, fluently, not as if you were interpreting from the French. No, it was more than that. You were so familiar with the text, it was as though you were the author and had spent years painstakingly working on it.

You read only two to three chapters each time. So I waited impatiently for the next date at Mei Nong, with you, and with the little prince.

I chuckled when you read:

If you tell grown-ups, "I saw a beautiful red brick house, with geraniums at the windows and doves on the roof," they won't be able to imagine such a house. You have to tell them, "I saw a house worth a hundred thousand francs." Then they exclaim, "What a pretty house!"

A sarcastic smile rose to your lips. But you never laughed out loud; only ripples of a grin flowed on your face.

You read the fox's words as if they were from the deepest of your dreams.

That pleasant voice of yours recited:

But if you tame me, my life will be filled with sunshine. I'll know the sound of footsteps that will be different from all the rest. Other footsteps send me back underground. Yours will call me out of my burrow like music. And then, look! You see the wheat fields over there? I don't eat bread. For me wheat is of no use whatever. Wheat fields say nothing to me. Which is sad. But you have hair the color of gold. So it will be wonderful, once you've tamed me! The wheat, which is golden, will remind me of you. And I'll love the sound of the wind in the wheat..."

I couldn't help but ask: "How do you tame the fox"?
You glanced at me and continued:

"You have to be very patient," the fox answered. "First you'll sit down a little way away from me, over there, in the grass. I'll watch you out of the corner of my eye, and you won't say anything. Language is the source of misunderstandings. But day by day, you'll be able to sit a little closer..."

I lowered my head and drank the already cold coffee to hide my tearing eyes.

When the little prince left, I cried like a baby – the first time I cried like that since I became an adult.

In tears, I saw that dusk had departed and the night arrived. Mr. Hu came up quietly to refill our cups and bring us a plate of cookies. I felt grateful to him for not turning on the light until he was ready to go downstairs, so my red eyes would not be seen.

No one else came upstairs that whole night. Thank goodness. We sat quietly, bathed in the inexpressible sweet sadness.

So I knew then that I would cry because of you some day. For the fox already told us this: you risk tears if you let yourself be tamed.

We started to find references to *The Little Prince* in our lives.

I'd say that I happened to meet a serious man at work. Then you'd laugh and say in a ridiculous voice: "I'm a serious man. I can't be bothered with trifles!"

You'd say that the fox is really a lovely friend. Its understanding of the emotional bond between people is truly imaginative. You didn't say anything after that. But I could hear you ruminating silently: "If you tame me, we'll need each other. To me, you're the only one. To you, I'm the only one…"

Both of us had the habit of asking for a glass of water when we ordered the coffee. We'd smile at each other when the water arrived because we thought of what the little prince said: "Water can also be good for your heart…"

And we'd agreed on a time to come to the café. For the fox said: "It would have been better to return at the same time… for instance, if you come at four in the afternoon, I'll begin to be happy by three. The closer it gets to four, the happier I'll feel."

These were the reasons.


I still don't know the secret ingredients of Mei Nong's coffee. I have heard that the exclusive recipe has been in Mr. Hu's family for generations – a popular tale amongst coffee lovers, which I have yet to confirm with Mr. Hu. Sometimes I will think of asking him before I come to Mei Nong and forget once I'm here. There are times when I want to ask while sipping coffee upstairs, but am too embarrassed to shout downstairs. "I'll just ask when I'm ready to leave," I think, but then the question slips from my mind again.

I don't believe Mr. Hu is being secretive, and the customers at Mei Nong seem to understand that the soul of this café is not merely the coffee. The coffee wouldn't taste the same if Mr. Hu didn't make it – even if you had the exclusive recipe. Mr. Hu started to drink coffee at a young age, influenced by his father. He opened up a café because he enjoys the process and he became the only one who could brew such a dense, rich cup of coffee. He couldn't quit then even if he wanted to. A 15-second variance in brewing time is all it takes for a hand poured coffee to be a success or a failure. A regular customer can tell the subtle differences right away. A love of coffee is innate – some people were born to bathe in coffee's aroma every day.

I couldn't drink coffee initially. I got stomach pain from just a little sip. So I only ordered black tea or juice, and enjoyed the scent of coffee when I was in a café. But the second time I was at Mei Nong, I forgot and ordered a cup of house coffee. It had a peculiar fragrance that reminded me of my time in college. I savored the coffee while contemplating you and your secrets.

When I realized my mistake, I had already finished the coffee. Strangely, I didn't get any stomach pain, not one bit. It must have been a combination of Mei Nong coffee, the reminiscence of my college time and imagining you that cured my sensitivity to coffee. I have no problem drinking it now.

I asked for your name.

"I have a terrible name. But my screen name is Snow Deep," you said.

I thought of my screen name, "Green Field". I was going to tell you but decided not to because of the two names belonging to different seasons.

I like your name. I experienced a snowstorm when I was little. We don't get much snow these days. Even if it does fall, the snow doesn't accumulate.

Snow Deep – sounds like a childish prayer or a cold crystal painting.

I asked about your work. You said you don't have any "job".

"How do you make a living then?" I said.

You told me you owned a small shop "Purely Handmade", selling commodities and artifacts from Tibet and Yunnan. Business wasn't great. You also crafted leather purses, bags, and luggage, as well as designing and making bracelets. You'll sell some of these when you are short of money.

You gave me a small leather pouch one day (my only present from you). It fits in my hand. I don't know what kind of leather it is, but it's soft. You dyed it the color of wine and stitched on blue and silver stars. A thin string was sewn at the mouth of the pouch. There were seven dark brown coffee beans inside, and each dimly shone with a sheen that was full and smooth. One side rounded, the other side flat with a deep groove, the coffee beans had a playful, animated look.

You told me these were dark roasted Mandheling beans from Sumatera Island. To me, they were seven brown, opaque precious gems.

I asked why you were giving me a present; it was not my birthday or any special occasion. You said the best day to give gifts was any day chosen by the gift giver. What a lovely explanation, and what a lovely present.

If I knew we'd be parted for a long time then, I would have been greedier and asked for more and better stuff. But then, what was the use of having those things if I couldn't be with you?

But I knew we were not like others. We didn't have a "thereafter" from the very beginning. Or maybe it was the other way around: our bonding started because we understood that a conventional ending was not for us.

We talked about marriage.

"Everyone has their own views on marriage, and mine is not to get married," you said, an attitude as light as a breeze gliding over the water on an early summer morning.

"Why?" I stopped short of saying. "No one can doubt that you'll be a good husband."

"Were you hurt by a woman?" I asked.

"Why? Do men like to use that excuse?" You choked and laughed out loud.

"But why, really?"

"If I like a woman, I want to spend time with her in a café. But no man will want to spend time with his wife in a café."

It took me all night to digest your thoughts. I wanted to refute them but didn't know what to say.

Really, I knew I was lucky, and I believed my good luck was a rare item in this city. I didn't ask for more. But if you hadn't stated your attitude so clearly, and let me at least satisfy my vanity a little, then things would have been perfect.

Though I knew long ago that in this world, perfection doesn't exist.

And I understood the other iron rule: anything that's special won't last long.

Be ordinary or be momentary. We don't have any other choice.

You said you were leaving the country, but didn't say when. All of a sudden, you disappeared.


Many things happened after you had gone – the 9/11 incident, the war in Afghanistan, the multiple plane crashes, the multiple mine accidents, the multiple terrorist attacks that spilled innocent blood. I didn't talk to anyone about these events, but felt them shoving and bullying me as they came at me from all directions. I tried to keep my balance but gave up because I was too confused and disoriented.

But there are some changes that newspaper and TV will not broadcast. They are tiny but important, and there is one which I must tell you: Mei Nong is about to be torn down.

The city's plan is to demolish the old houses along Nanking Road, either at the end of this year or the beginning of next year.

Anxious, I asked Mr. Hu what to do.

"I'm getting old anyway, I don't need to continue. I'm happy that I've made so many friends here. It's not a big deal that the shop is going to close down. You can all come to my house when you want a good cup of coffee, no charge."

That can't be. It's not only me; all of the regular customers say so. Everybody likes Mei Nong, more than any other stylish café. We like it for its nostalgia and easy-going presence. We like that it's far away from the city's buzzing atmosphere. We like that the owner brews coffee not to make money but to make friends.

Mei Nong and its customers tame each other.

No one wants Mei Nong to close down. But Mr. Hu is only a renter. He doesn't have any way to continue the business on his own. You know, for all these years, he didn't make much money off this place.

For a while, we were all a bit worried. But then the good news came. One of the customers who loves Mei Nong coffee will buy a house for Mr. Hu to keep Mei Nong open, with no rental charges.

We formed a club and everyone became a member. There was no member fee – you just had to donate a chair with the donor's name on it. Limited to one.

"I'm in," I said right away.

"Count me in." "And me." "Me too!"

"It's not final yet. No hurry," said Mr. Hu calmly.

We lost touch when you left the country.

I know you meant it to be this way, and I think I know why. To use coffee as an analogy: the aroma of coffee being ground is better than that of coffee being brewed. And the aroma of brewed coffee is more delicious than when coffee is being consumed. When drinking the coffee, the first sip always tastes better than the last. So you never really want to finish that final drop.

But aren't you lonely for always being this way? Does it taste like a cup of strong black coffee, this loneliness that you cannot confide to anyone, so bitter that your heart trembles? I won't argue if you say you like this feeling, but I'll never believe it either.

You'll come back for sure. Some night, you'll stay in a café in a foreign land until closing time. You'll put up the chair on the table, look at the surroundings, walk out backward, and then go directly to the airport. You've been living in an alien place for too long. You must have dreamed about Shanghai's cafés. You'll come back, for certain.

Once you're off the airplane, you'll come directly to Mei Nong – if you're not too tired.

If you're really beat, you'll fall into sleep first, deep, as if you were dead. It's not possible to sleep like this when you are all by yourself in a foreign place. And when you're awake, you'll be at a loss for a few moments, for you'll not be sure where you are and what you should do next. Then you decide to come to Mei Nong to find your bearings.

In any case, you'll come to Mei Nong soon after you come back. Mei Nong is a place we cannot part with. It's what makes this city different than any other. Of this I am sure, just as I am sure the snow will fall to the ground.

Snow Deep, if you're drifting in the air, I'll quietly wait for you to sink down.

You're a man who lives according to your heart's desire. But the changes of the world sometimes shake up that heart. You'll not have imagined that Mei Nong could be demolished. Will you be disoriented all of a sudden, like waking up from a deep dream and facing a totally strange, unimaginable environment? Will you feel like you've fallen into a dream within your dream?

There's a chance I might miss you entirely, and it's getting worse by the day because I don't know when Mei Nong will be torn down, or when you'll be back. Mei Nong might be gone when you return. And if you come here, all you'll see is ruins.

But don't feel desperate; don't be sentimental about the past just yet. There is a moving note on the remaining wall where customers can find a map and address for the new Mei Nong.

Mei Nong's small green store sign is still there. And you'll see the familiar café name is covered by a message I left for you, written with a large Mitsubishi paint pen.

Only one sentence. I do not know what else to say to you.

If you see it, you'll come to the new Mei Nong for sure.

And you'll see, as you enter through the door, that Mr. Hu has not changed a bit. He'll say to you, "Haven't seen you for so long," and then let you sit in a chair made of walnut wood and sand-colored leather, as pretty as your handcrafted goods. It's roomy and comfortable.

Mr. Hu will say, "This is your chair."

You'll not be surprised, or rather you will not have enough time to be surprised. Because you'll see that on the back of the chair are the words "Snow Deep". You'll understand.

And then, if you want to know my name, you can look at the chair opposite yours.

I had been meaning to keep silent, but I'm worried that if Mei Nong were to be torn down too early, or if you came too late, there would be nothing left at the original location. So I wrote all this down, hoping you'd see it.

And what I wrote on the sign of the old café was this: "Snow Deep, I'll be waiting for you at Mei Nong."

*Translated by Jennie Chu*
All quotations are from Richard Howard's translation
of *The Little Prince* by Antoine De Saint-Exupery

# Translators

*Eric Abrahamsen*

Eric is the founder of Paper Republic, a website introducing Chinese literature to English-speaking audiences. His translation publications include Xu Zechen's Running Through Beijing, for which he received a NEA grant, and which was short-listed for the National Translation Award; he also received a PEN translation grant for Wang Xiaobo's My Spiritual Homeland. His short-story translations have appeared in magazines including The New Yorker and Granta.

*Dylan Levi King*

Dylan Levi King is a translator and writer based in Tokyo. His most recent project is Dong Xi's Record of Regret (University of Oklahoma Press, 2018).

*Canaan Morse*

*Canaan Morse was one of the founding editors of Pathlight: New Chinese Writing. He is a literary translator and editor with an M.A. in Classical Chinese Literature from Peking University. His work has appeared in The Kenyon Review, Chinese Literature Today, Cha: An Asian Literary Journal, Words and the World, and elsewhere. His translation of Ge Fei's novella The Invisibility Cloak, which won the Susan Sontag Prize for Translation, is due for publication in 2015 by New York Review of Books, as part of the NYRB Classics Series. He lives in Maine.*

*Roddy Flagg*

*Roddy Flagg accidentally moved to China after graduating in something entirely irrelevant, and surprised himself by ending up earning a living translating Chinese and running websites. He left China after ten years and is now living in Edinburgh, where he continues to surprise himself.*

*Ken Liu*

*Ken Liu (http://kenliu.name) is an author of speculative fiction, as well as a translator, lawyer, and programmer. A winner of the Nebula, Hugo, and World Fantasy awards, he is the author of The Dandelion Dynasty, a silkpunk epic fantasy series ( The Grace of Kings (2015), The Wall of Storms (2016), and a forthcoming third volume) and The Paper Menagerie and Other Stories (2016), a collection. He also wrote the Star Wars novel, The Legends of Luke Skywalker (2017). In addition to his original fiction, Ken also translated numerous works from Chinese to English, including The Three-Body Problem (2014), by Liu Cixin, and "Folding Beijing," by Hao Jingfang, both Hugo winners.*

*Jennie Chia-Hui Chu*

*Jennie Chia-Hui Chu is a writer and a translator based in Boston, Massachusetts. Her writing and translations have appeared in print and online, with publications such as Asymptote, The Boston Globe Magazine, Brevity, The Christian Science Monitor, The Literary Review, Pathlight Megazine, and the World Journal. Two of her essays were recorded by NPR's All Things Considered.*

*Poppy Toland*

*Poppy Toland is a London-based writer, editor and literary translator.*

# THE HOT SPRINGS
# ON MOON MOUNTAIN

新时代纪事丛书
## TALES OF NEW ERA SERIES

### 编委会
### Editorial Committee

**主任委员** / 施战军 胡开敏
**Chairman:** Shi Zhanjun, Hu Kaimin

**委员** / 施战军 胡开敏 徐明强 艾瑞克 徐则臣
程异 陈冬梅 曾惠杰 李兰玉 大卫 曹禅 莫楷 刘欣
**Commissioner:** Shi Zhanjun, Hu Kaimin, Xu Mingqiang, Eric Abrahamsen,
Xu Zechen, Jeremy Tiang, Chen Dongmei, Zeng Huijie, Li Lanyu,
Dave Haysom, Karmia Olutade, Canaan Morse, Alice Xin Liu

**编辑总监** / 艾瑞克 徐则臣
**Editorial Directors:** Eric Abrahamsen, Xu Zechen

**执行编辑** / 李兰玉
**Managing Editor:** Li Lanyu

**协作** / 纸托邦有限公司
With Paper Republic LLC, USA

**平面设计** / 北京午夜阳光平面设计公司
**Layout Design:** Beijing WYYG Graphic Design

**设计总监** / 王焱
**Art Director:** Wang Yan

**图书在版编目（CIP）数据**

月亮的温泉：英文 /《人民文学》编辑部主编 .
-- 北京：外文出版社，2022.9
（新时代纪事丛书）
ISBN 978-7-119-13189-4

Ⅰ.①月… Ⅱ.①人…
Ⅲ.①中国文学－当代文学－作品综合集－英文 Ⅳ.① I217.1
中国版本图书馆 CIP 数据核字 (2022) 第 178388 号


出版指导　胡开敏　施战军


责任编辑　曾惠杰
英文翻译　艾瑞克　程　昇　等
英文审订　徐明强
装帧设计　北京凤焦图文设计工作室
印刷监制　秦　蒙　王　争

## 月亮的温泉

《人民文学》编辑部　主编

© 2023 外文出版社有限责任公司
**出 版 人**　胡开敏
**出版发行**　外文出版社有限责任公司
**地　　址**　北京市西城区百万庄大街 24 号　　　**邮政编码**　100037
**网　　址**　http://www.flp.com.cn　　　　　　　**电子邮箱**　flp@cipg.org.cn
**电　　话**　008610-68320579（总编室）　　　　008610-68996177（编辑部）
　　　　　　　008610-68995852（发行部）　　　　008610-68996183（投稿电话）
**印　　刷**　北京侨友印刷有限公司
**经　　销**　新华书店 / 外文书店
**开　　本**　787mm×1092mm　1/16　　　　　　**印　张**　14.25
**版　　次**　2023 年 3 月 第 1 版第 1 次印刷　　　**字　数**　160 千字
　（英文）
**书　　号**　ISBN 978-7-119-13189-4
　（平）
11800